Elinor Wonders Why™

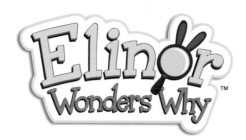

Hiding in Plain Sight

From an episode of the animated TV series *Elinor Wonders Why*, produced by SHOE Ink, LLC

Elinor Wonders Why © 2020 SHOE Ink, LLC

Adapted by Jennifer Stokes and Genie MacLeod, based on the TV episode "Hiding in Plain Sight,"
written by Tom Berger.

Book adaptation and realization © 2022 Kids Can Press

Published in Canada and the U.S. by Kids Can Press Ltd.
25 Dockside Drive, Toronto, ON M5A 0B5

Kids Can Press is a Corus Entertainment Inc. company

www.kidscanpress.com

The artwork in this book was rendered digitally.
The text is set in Elinor.

Edited by Genie MacLeod
Designed by Michael Reis

Printed and bound in Shenzhen, China, in 3/2022 by C & C Offset

CM 22 0 9 8 7 6 5 4 3 2 1

Library and Archives Canada Cataloguing in Publication

Title: Elinor wonders why, hiding in plain sight / created by Jorge Cham and Daniel Whiteson.
Other titles: Hiding in plain sight | Elinor wonders why (Television program)
Names: Cham, Jorge, author. | Whiteson, Daniel, author.
Identifiers: Canadiana 20210352639 | ISBN 9781525306198 (hardcover)
Subjects: LCSH: Camouflage (Biology) — Juvenile literature. | LCSH: Mimicry
(Biology) — Juvenile literature.
Classification: LCC QL767 .C53 2022 | DDC j591.47/2 — dc23

Kids Can Press gratefully acknowledges that the land on which our office is located is the
traditional territory of many nations, including the Mississaugas of the Credit, the Anishnabeg,
the Chippewa, the Haudenosaunee and the Wendat peoples, and is now home to many
diverse First Nations, Inuit and Métis peoples.

We thank the Government of Ontario, through Ontario Creates for supporting our publishing activity.

Hiding in Plain Sight

Created by Jorge Cham and Daniel Whiteson

Kids Can Press

Elinor

Elinor is curious about *everything*: Why do birds have feathers? How do flowers attract bees? How tall is the tallest tree? Questions like these lead Elinor and her friends on *big* adventures. By asking questions, making observations and testing out her ideas, Elinor unravels the mysteries of nature!

Olive

Olive always has her trunk in a book. She loves big words and has an excellent memory for interesting facts — elephants never forget, you know! A careful notetaker, too, Olive helps her friends make connections and solve nature's riddles.

Ari

Ari is a joker who loves making his friends laugh. When he's not clowning around, he's great at looking at problems from all sides (especially upside down!). Sometimes he'll even take to the skies to help his friends find the answers to their questions.

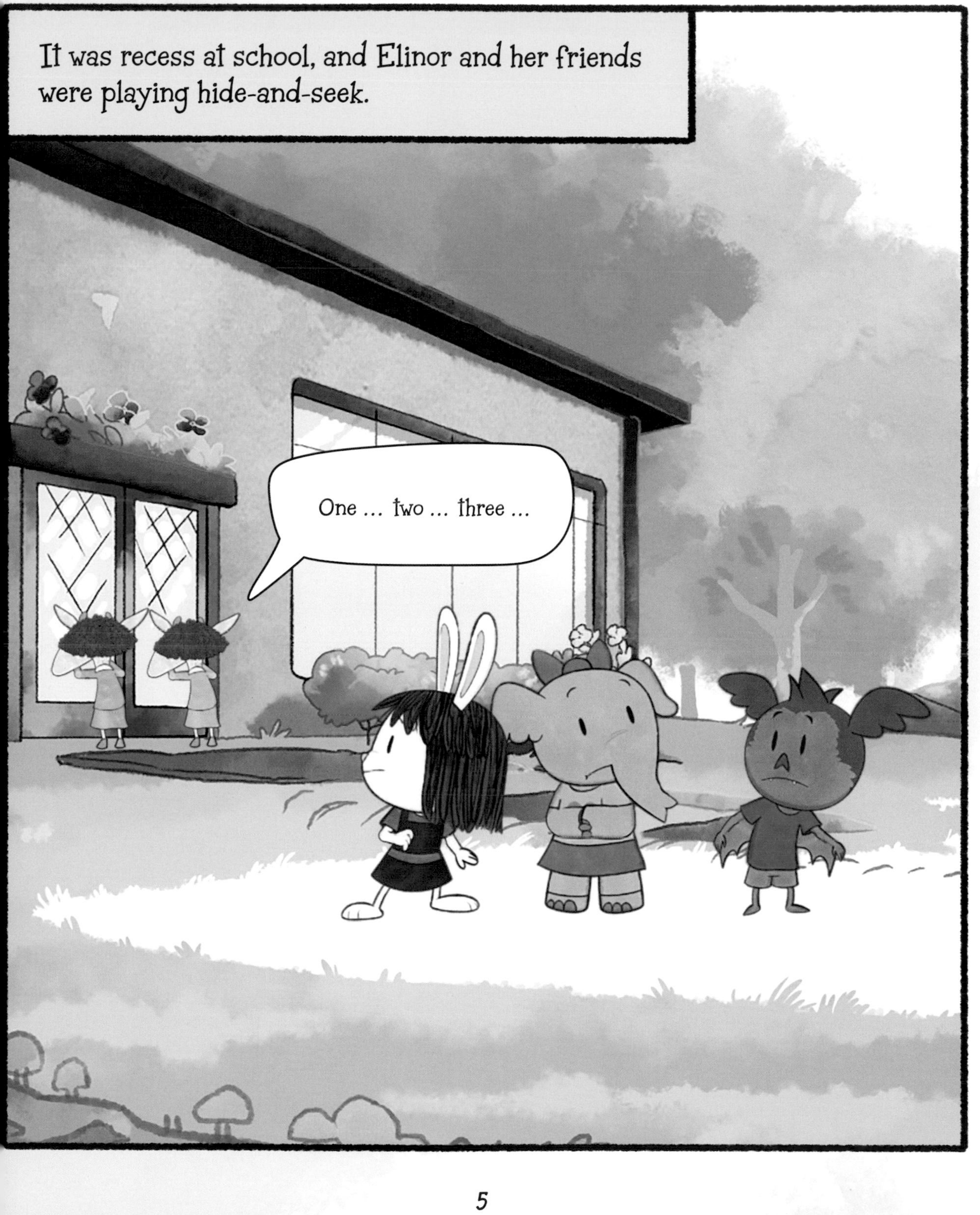
It was recess at school, and Elinor and her friends were playing hide-and-seek.
One ... two ... three ...

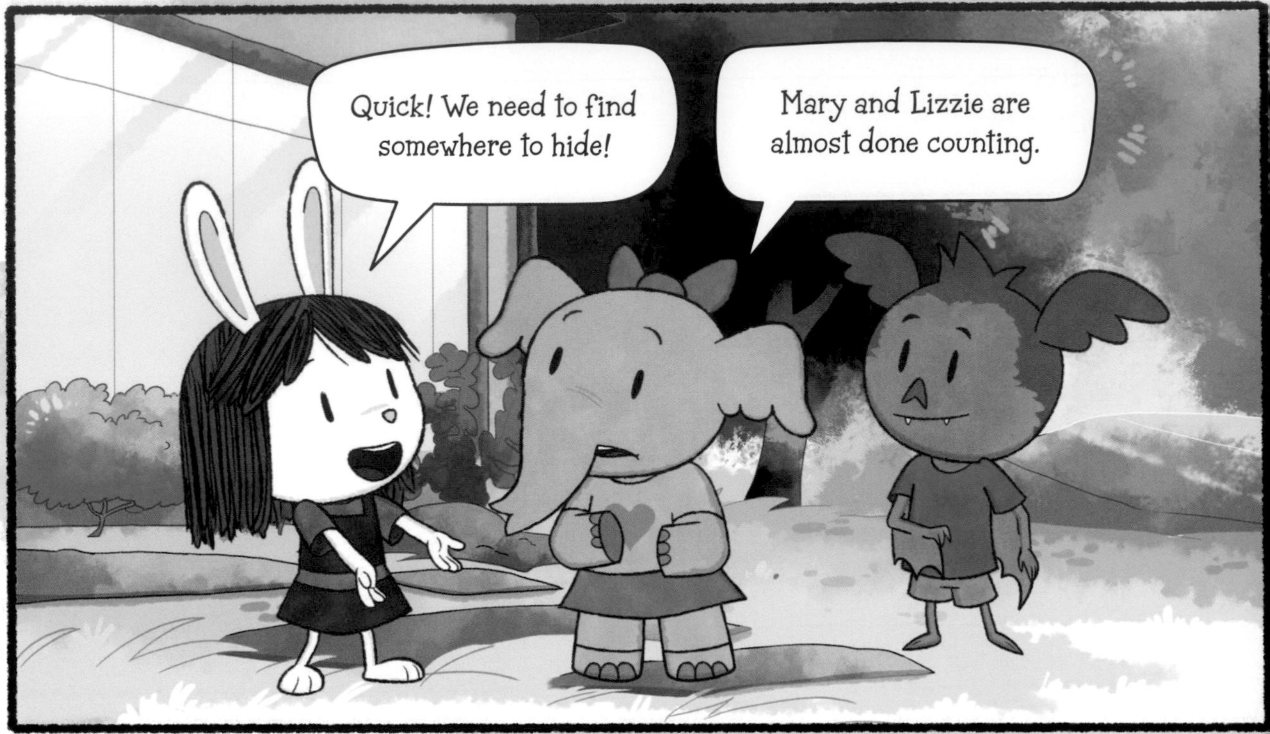
Quick! We need to find somewhere to hide!
Mary and Lizzie are almost done counting.

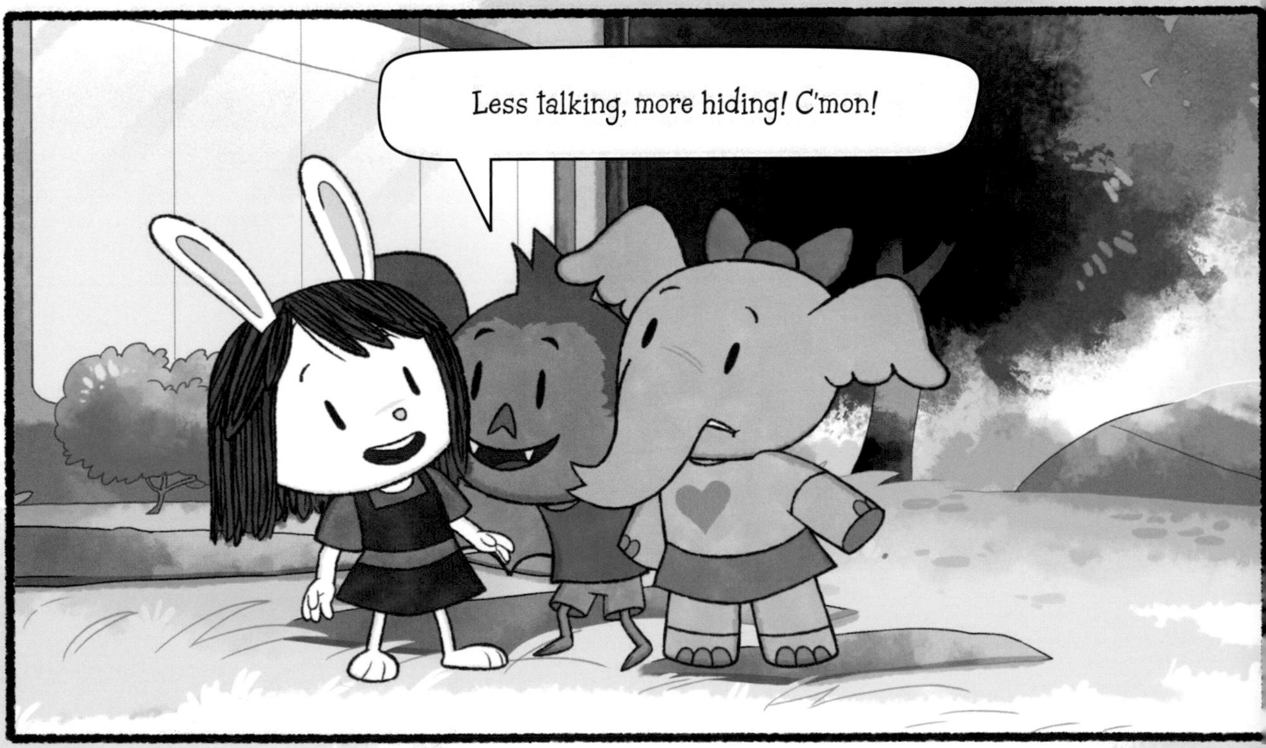
Less talking, more hiding! C'mon!

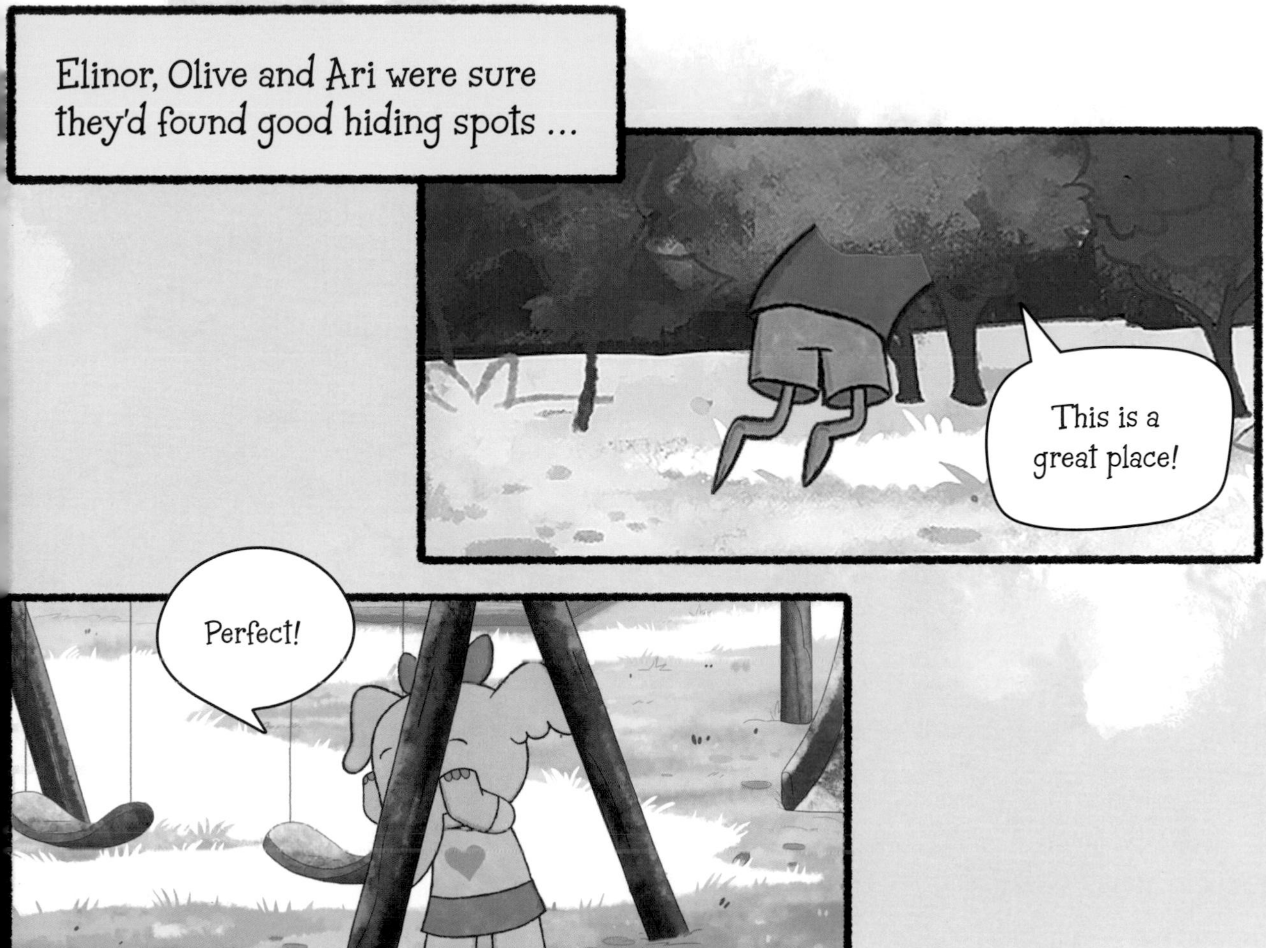
Elinor, Olive and Ari were sure they'd found good hiding spots ...
This is a great place!
Perfect!
Mary and Lizzie won't find me here!

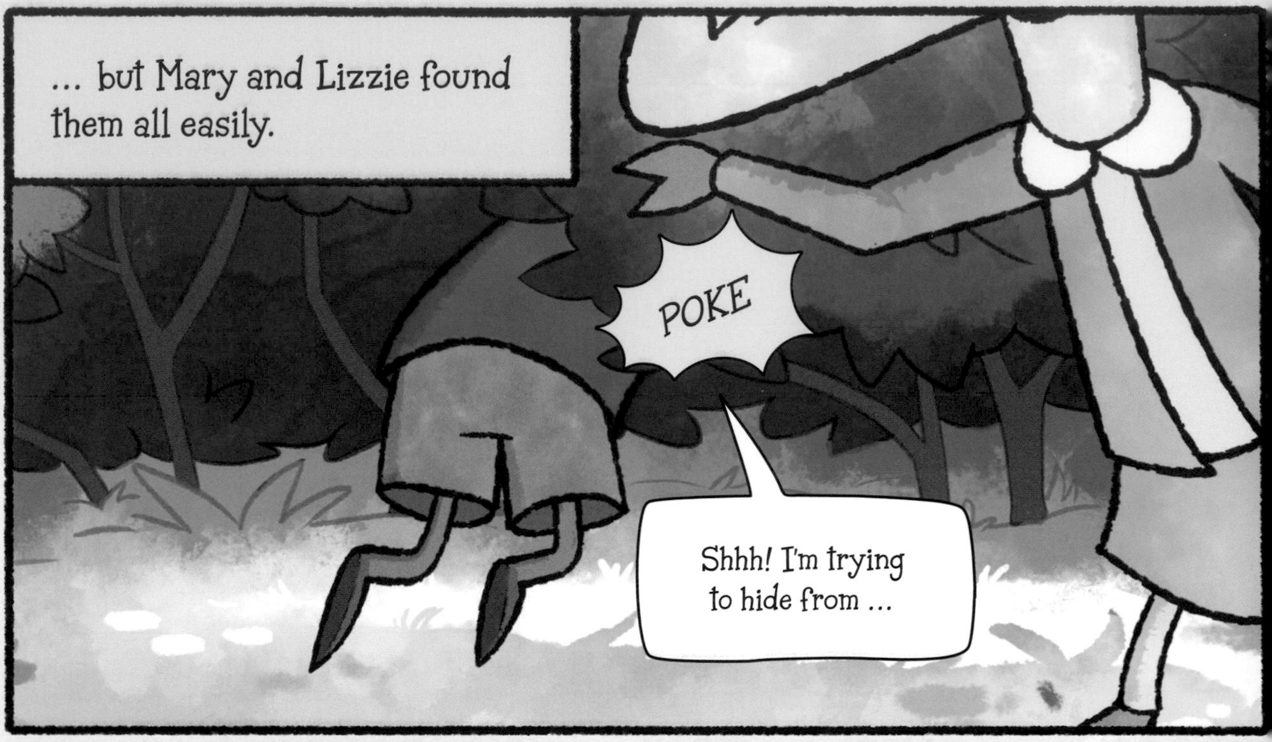
... but Mary and Lizzie found them all easily.
POKE
Shhh! I'm trying to hide from ...

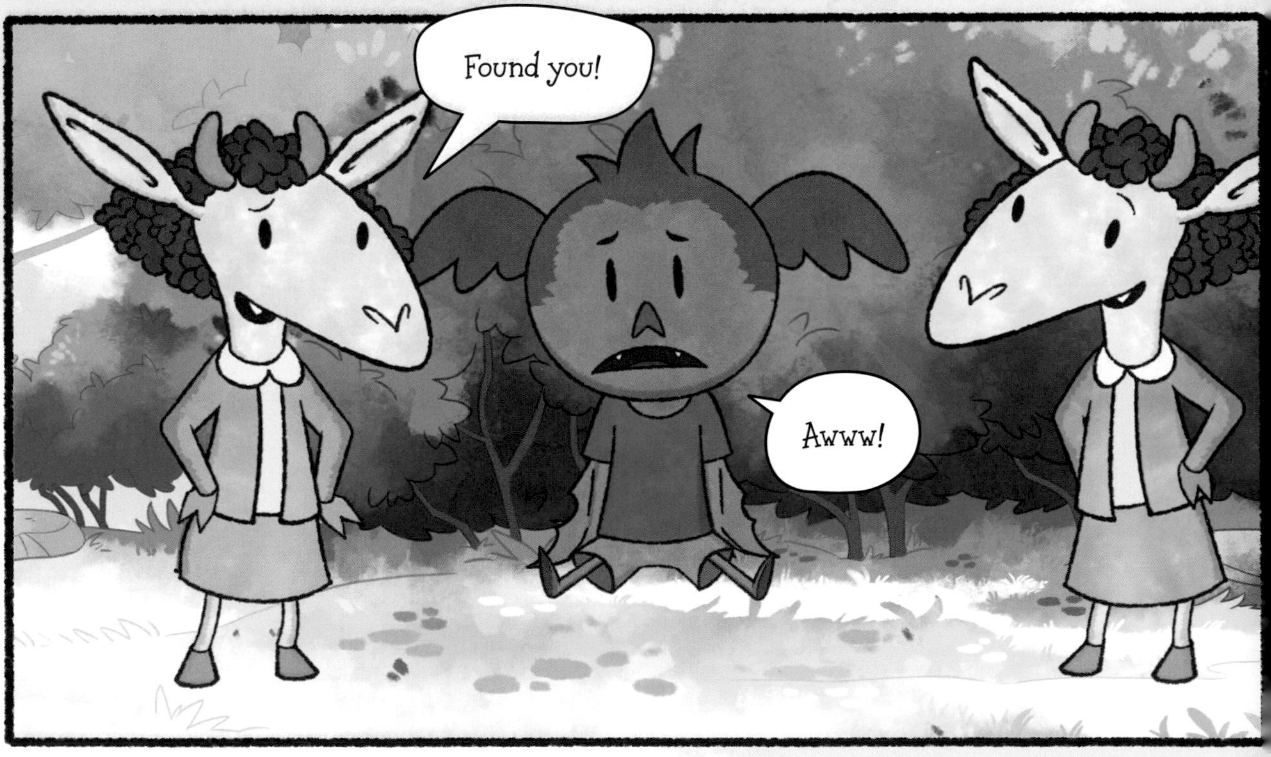
Found you!
Awww!

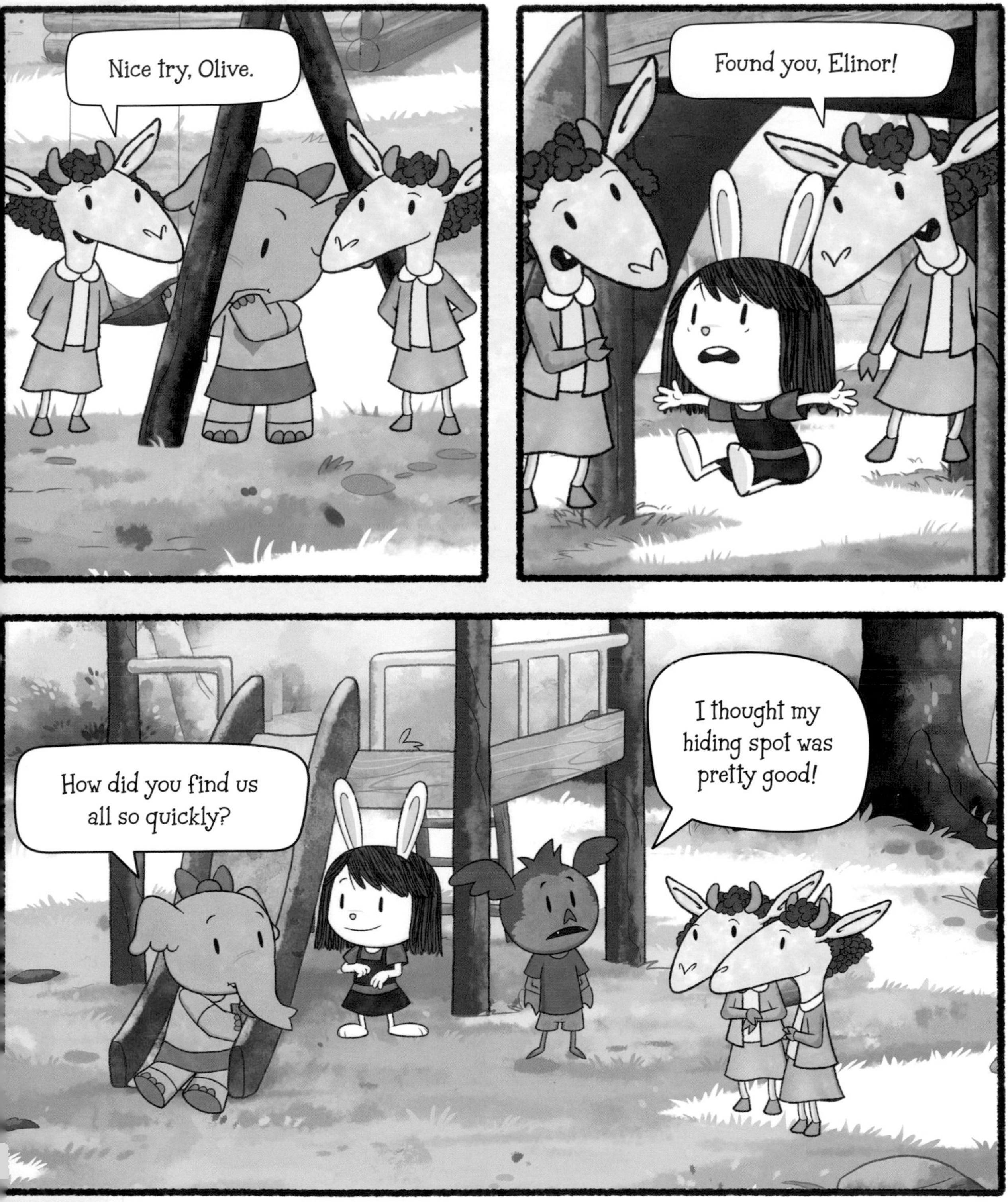
Nice try, Olive.
Found you, Elinor!
How did you find us all so quickly?
I thought my hiding spot was pretty good!

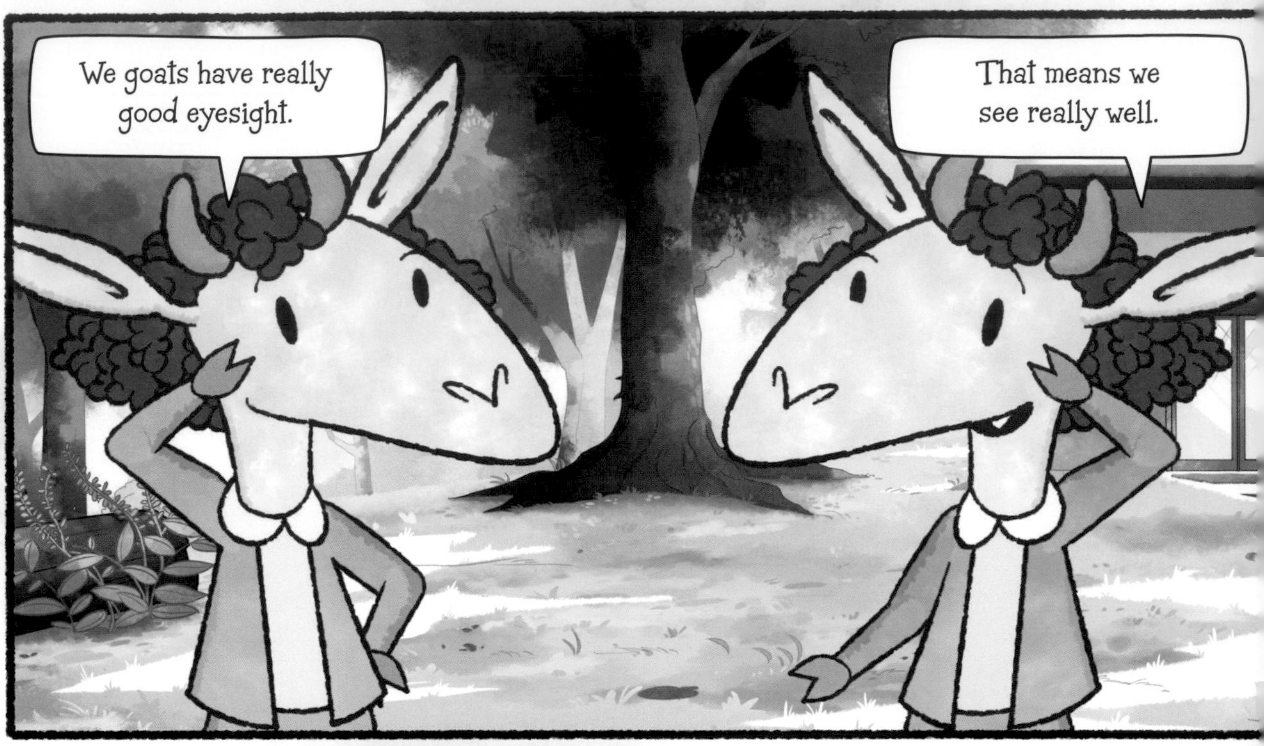
We goats have really good eyesight.
That means we see really well.

Let's Find Out!

Goats have special eyes that help them stay away from dangerous animals like coyotes. Goats' eyes can see very far from side to side and up and down. This helps them spot coyotes from far away and run to safety before the danger gets too close!

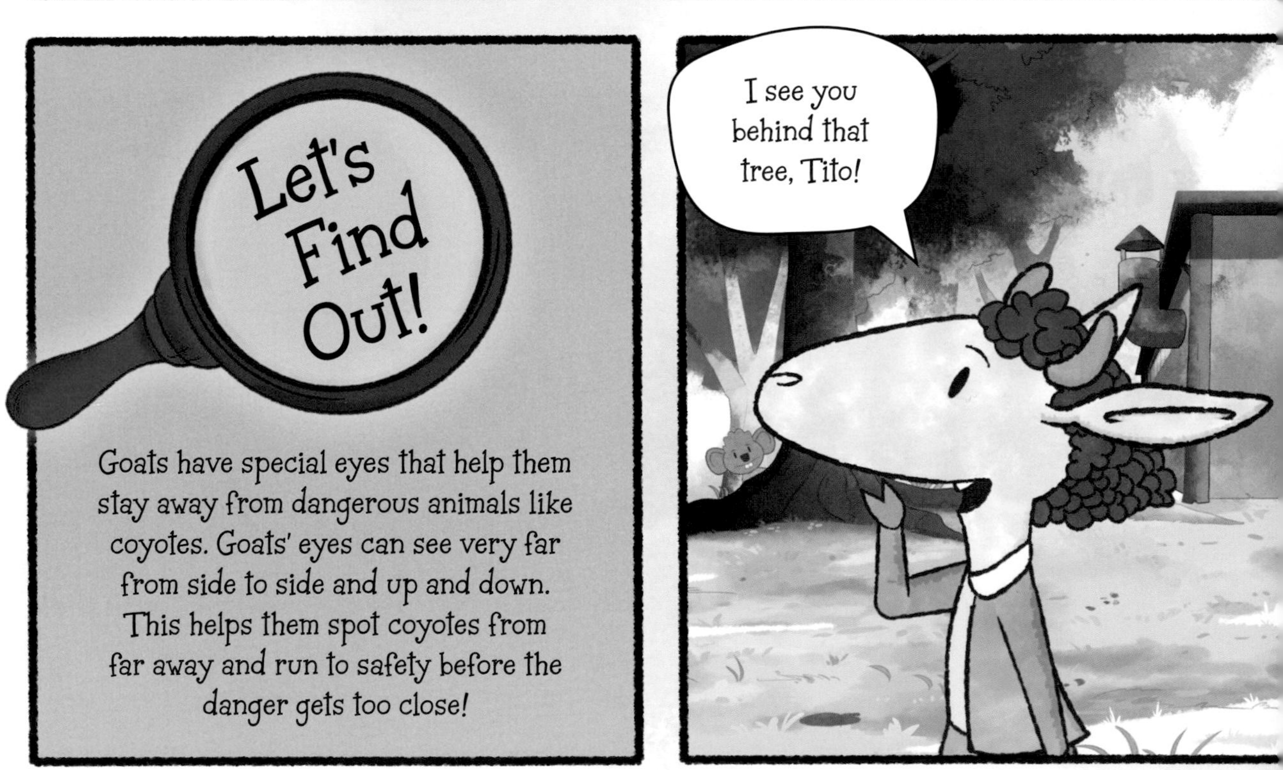
I see you behind that tree, Tito!

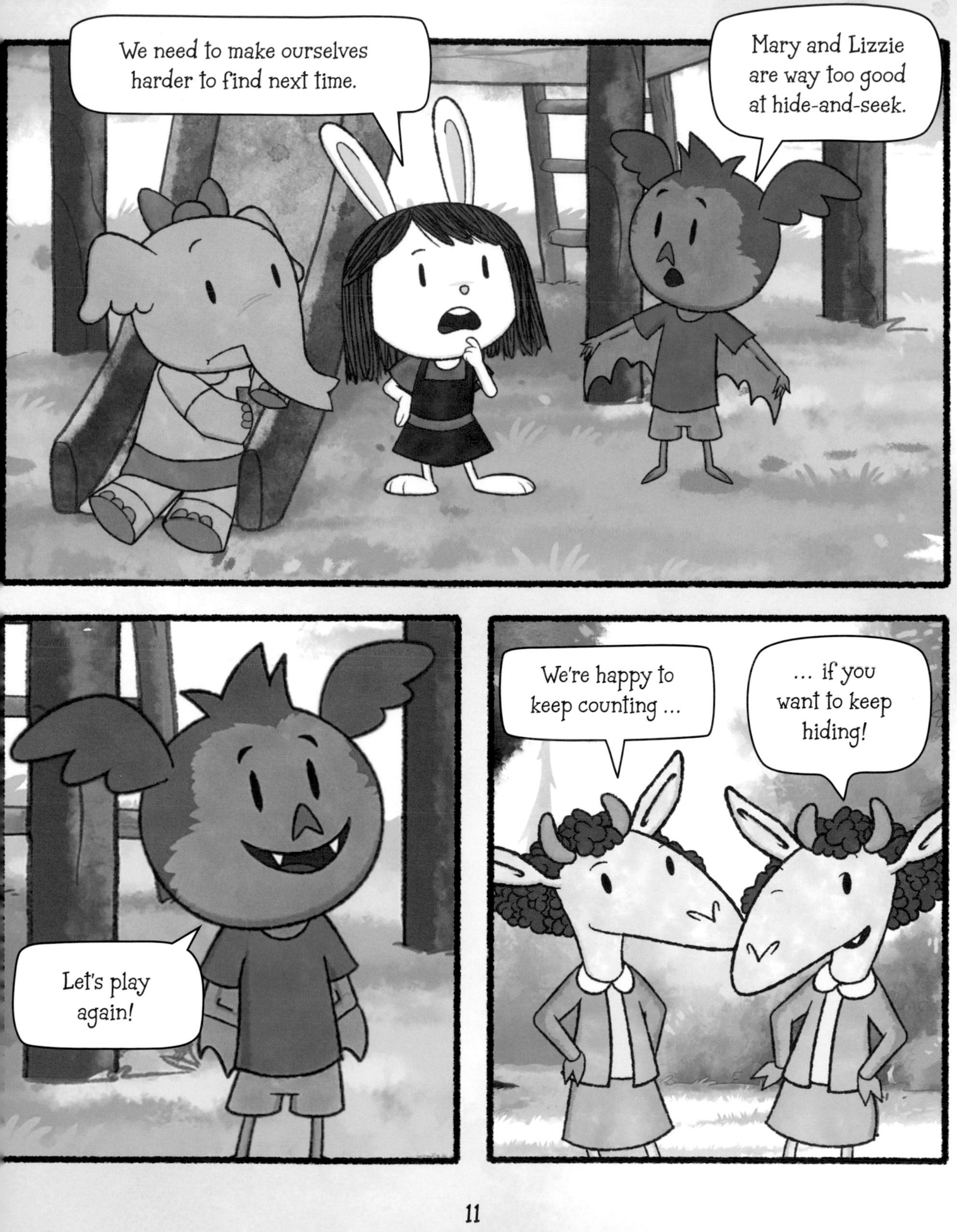
We need to make ourselves harder to find next time.
Mary and Lizzie are way too good at hide-and-seek.
Let's play again!
We're happy to keep counting ...
... if you want to keep hiding!

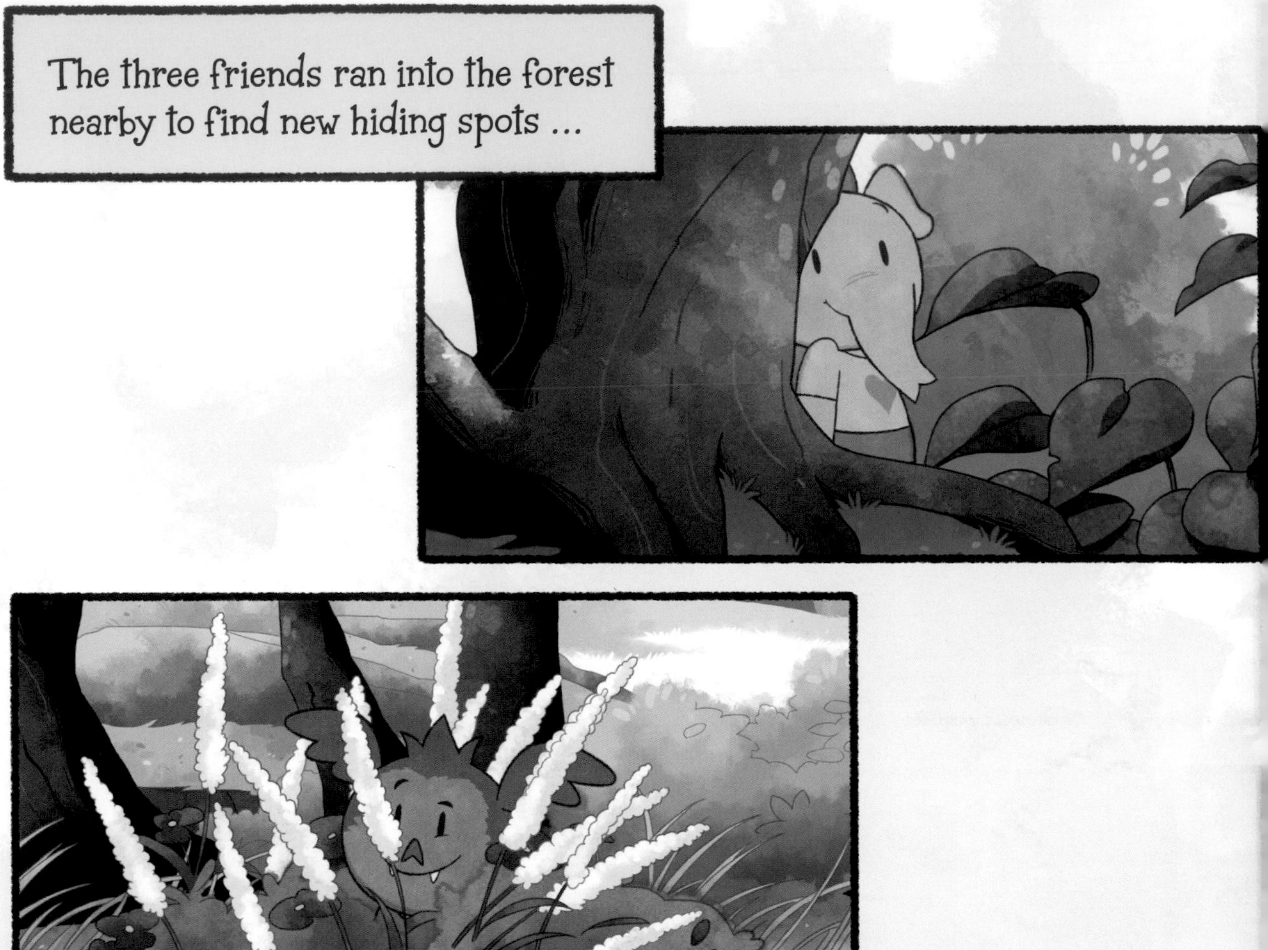
The three friends ran into the forest nearby to find new hiding spots ...

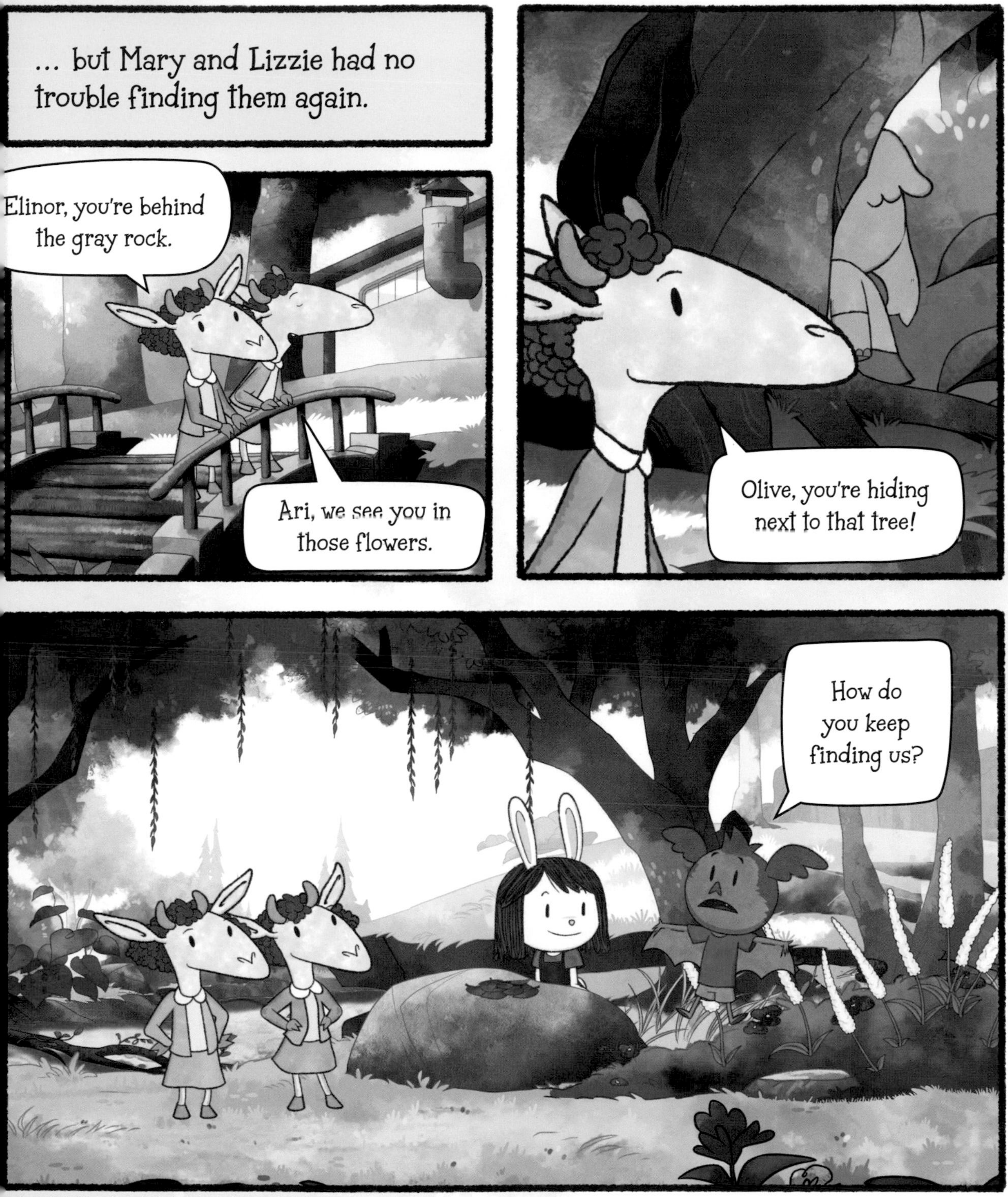
... but Mary and Lizzie had no trouble finding them again.
Elinor, you're behind the gray rock.
Ari, we see you in those flowers.
Olive, you're hiding next to that tree!
How do you keep finding us?

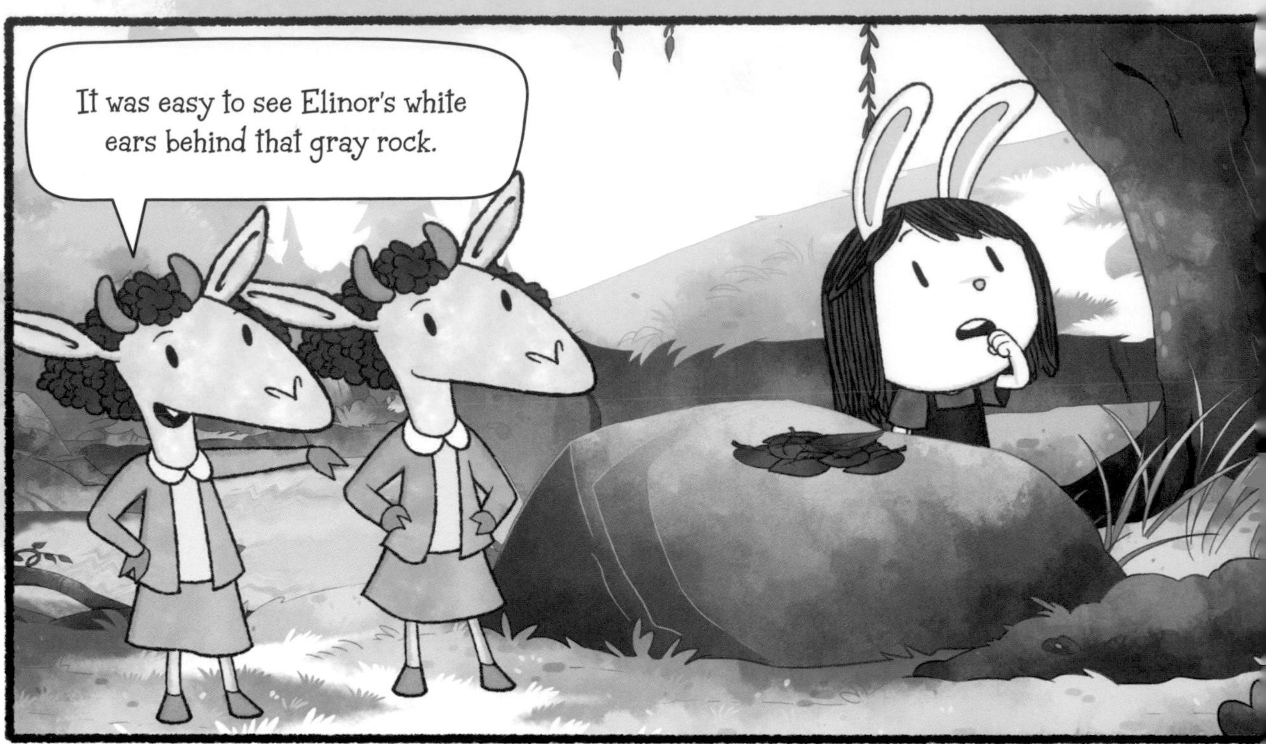
It was easy to see Elinor's white ears behind that gray rock.

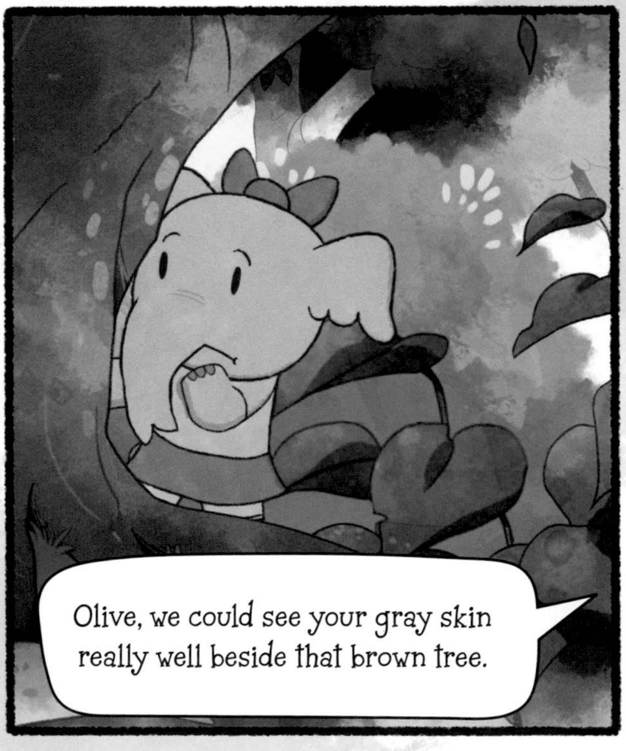
Olive, we could see your gray skin really well beside that brown tree.

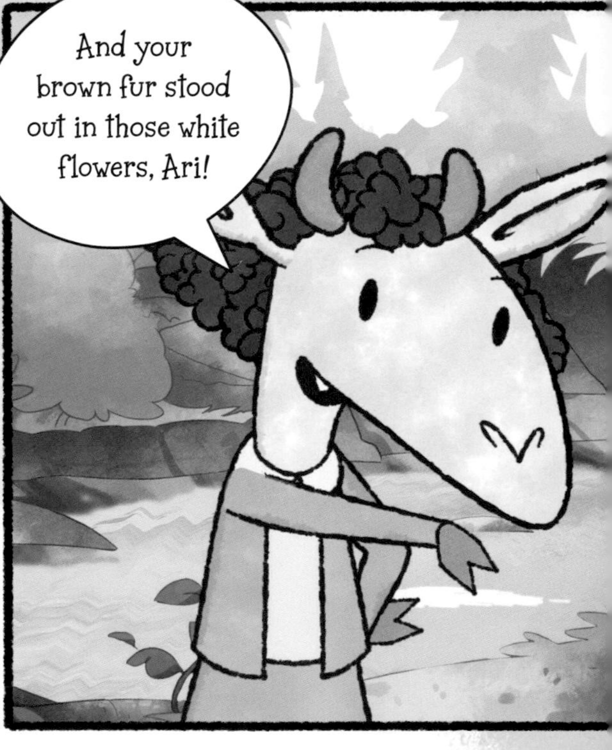
And your brown fur stood out in those white flowers, Ari!

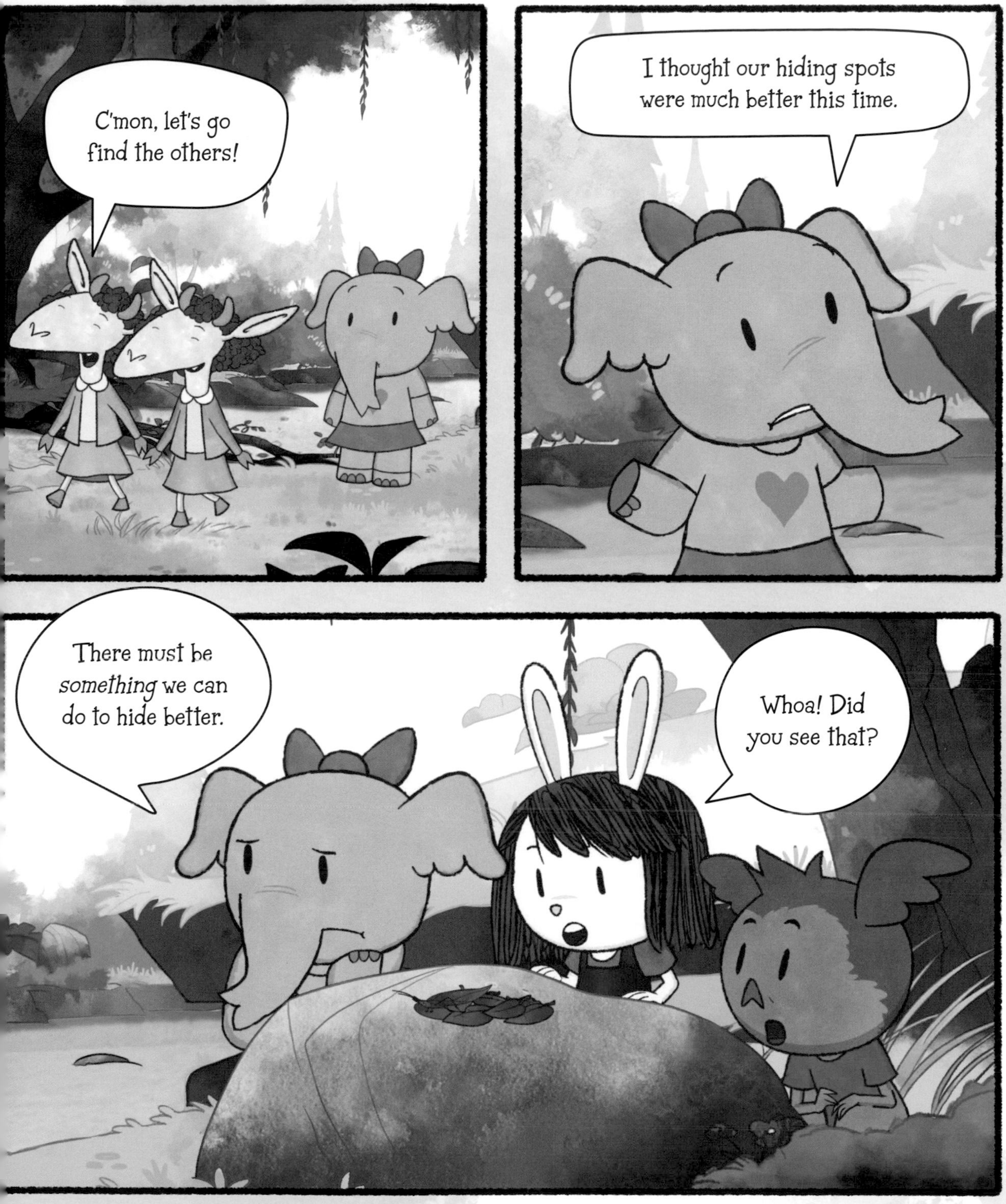
C'mon, let's go find the others!
I thought our hiding spots were much better this time.
There must be *something* we can do to hide better.
Whoa! Did you see that?

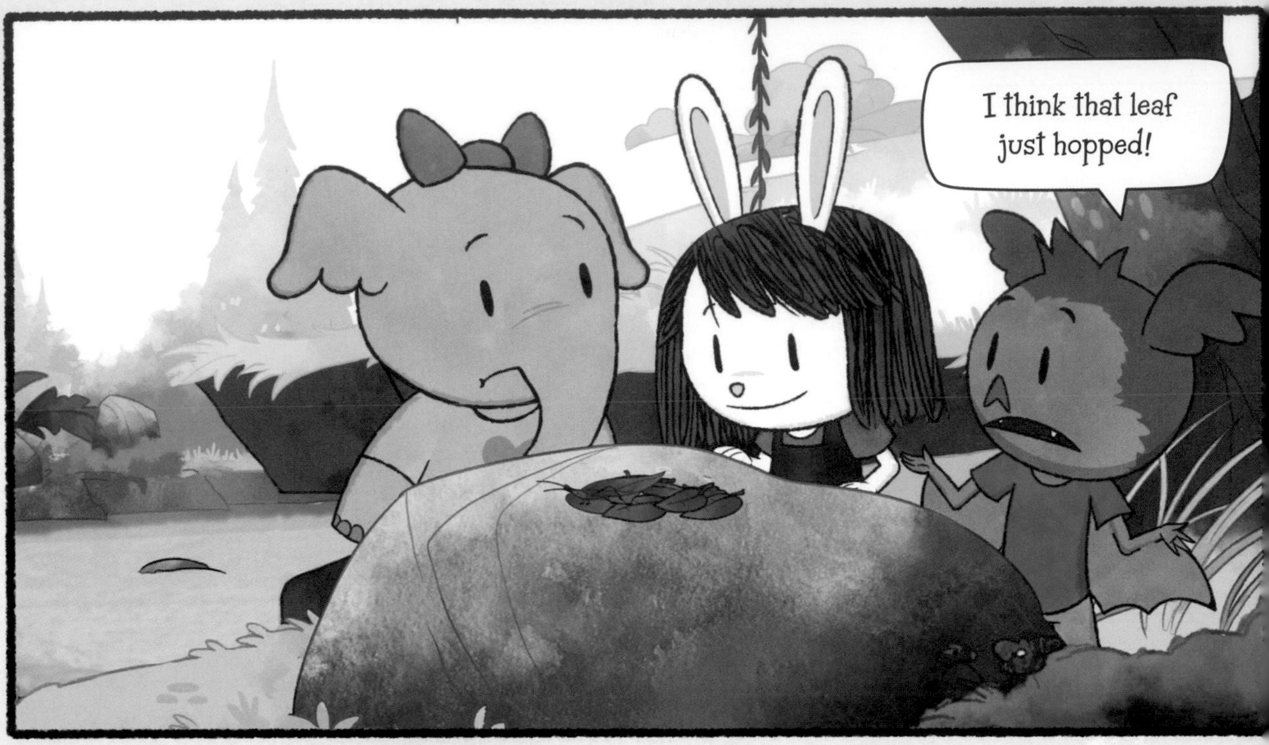
I think that leaf just hopped!

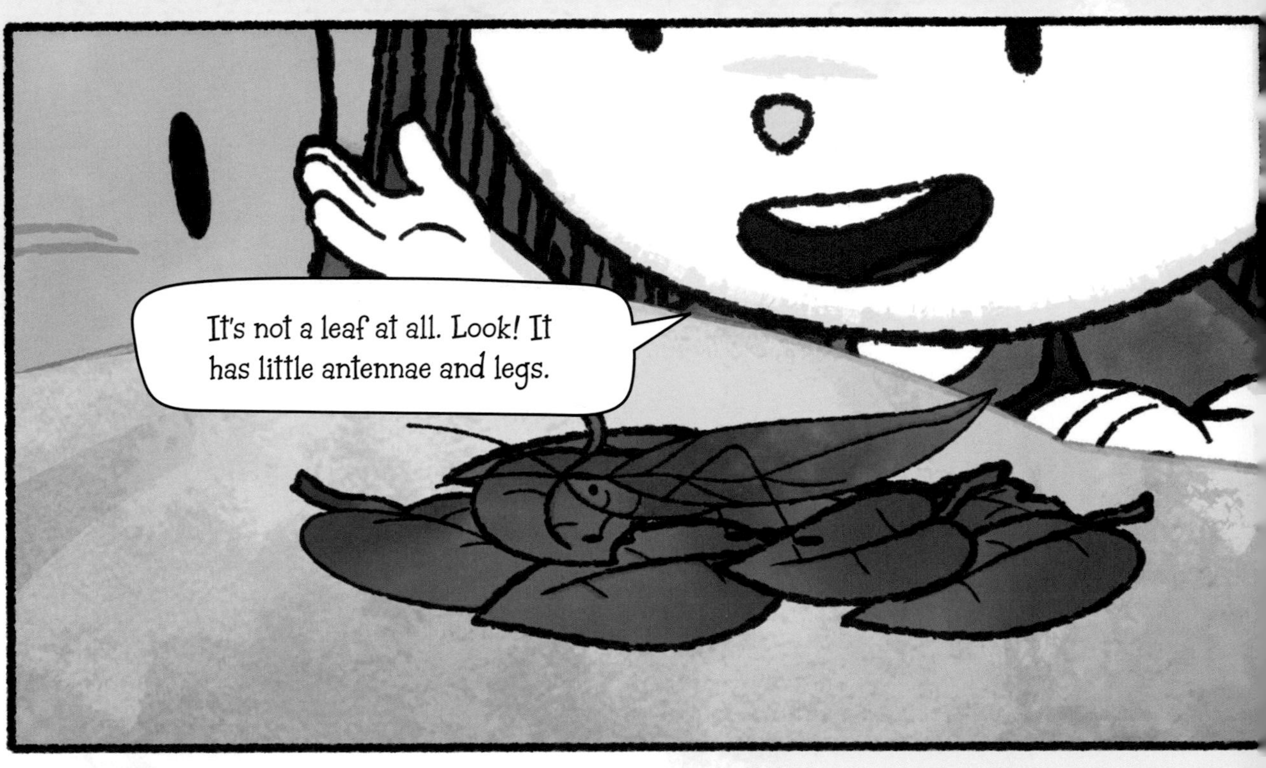
It's not a leaf at all. Look! It has little antennae and legs.

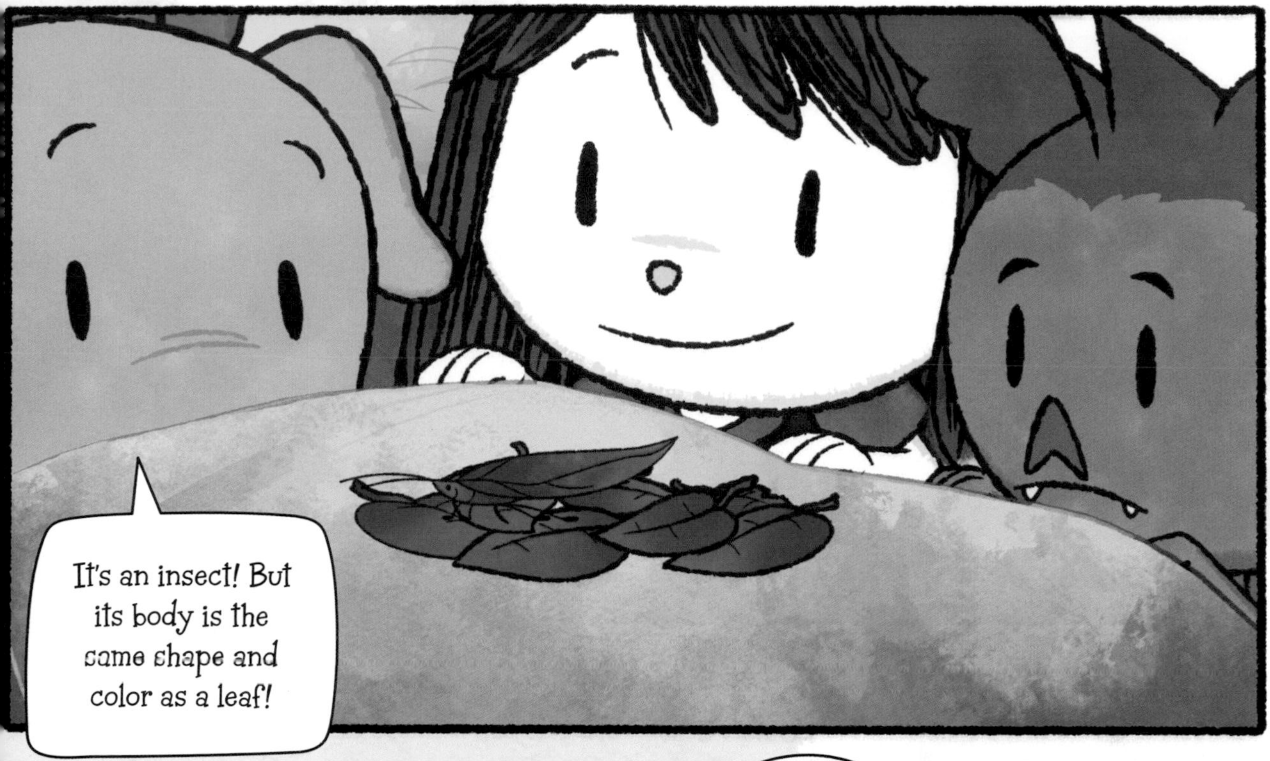
It's an insect! But its body is the same shape and color as a leaf!

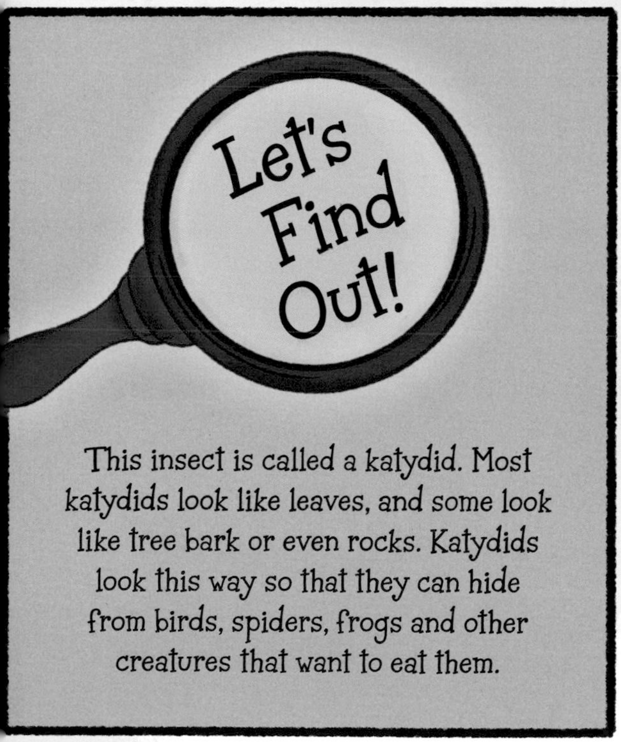
Let's Find Out!
This insect is called a katydid. Most katydids look like leaves, and some look like tree bark or even rocks. Katydids look this way so that they can hide from birds, spiders, frogs and other creatures that want to eat them.

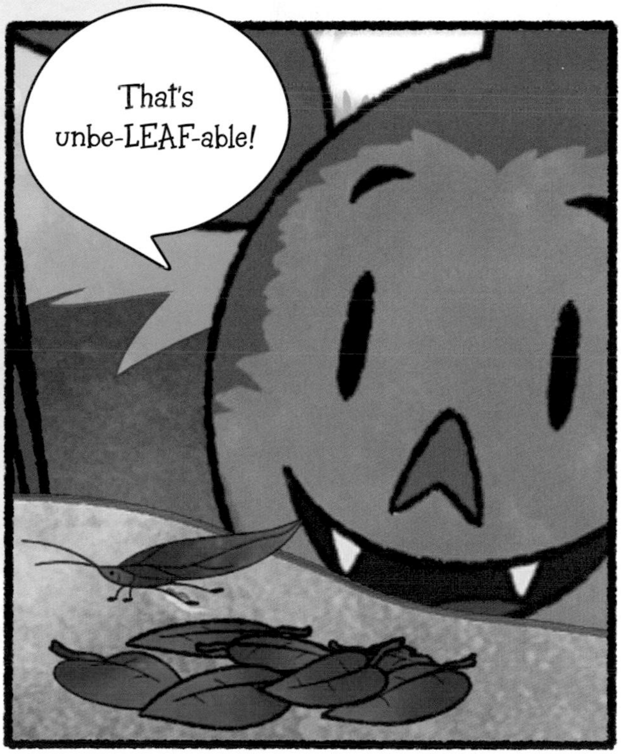
That's unbe-LEAF-able!

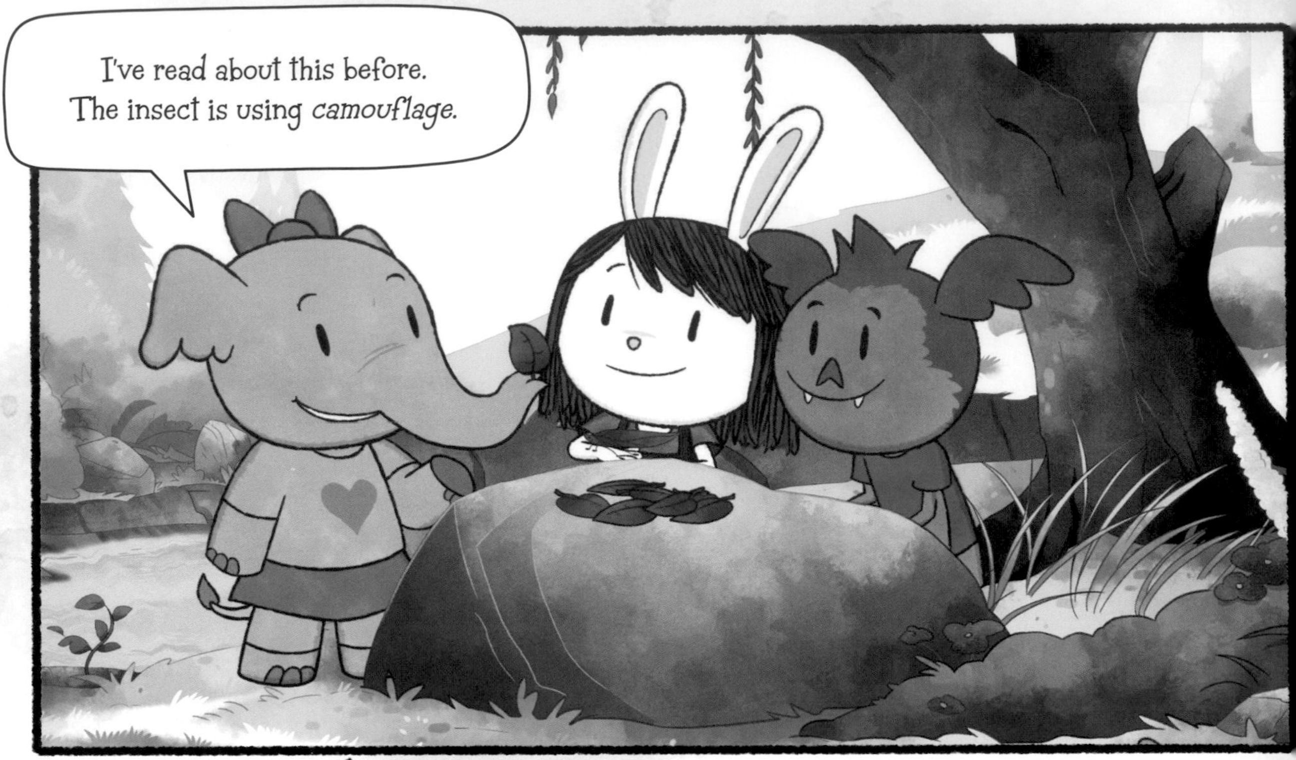
I've read about this before.
The insect is using *camouflage.*

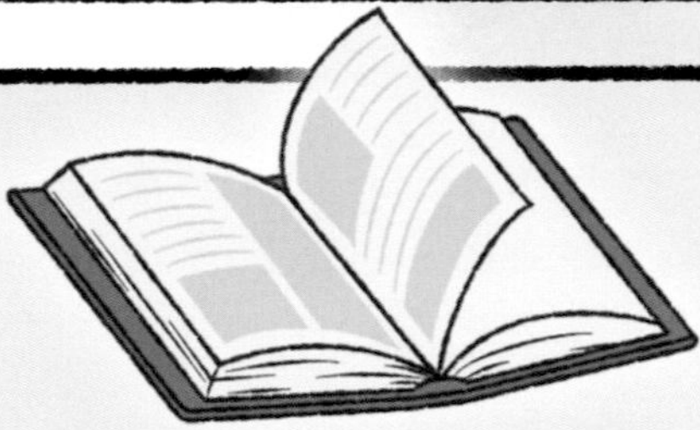

What's That Word?

Camouflage (KA-muh-flahj): A way of using colors, patterns, shapes and movement to blend in with the things around you. Camouflage helps some animals hide from dangers, and other animals sneak up on their next meal! Some animals naturally look like the things around them, and other animals blend in by changing their color.

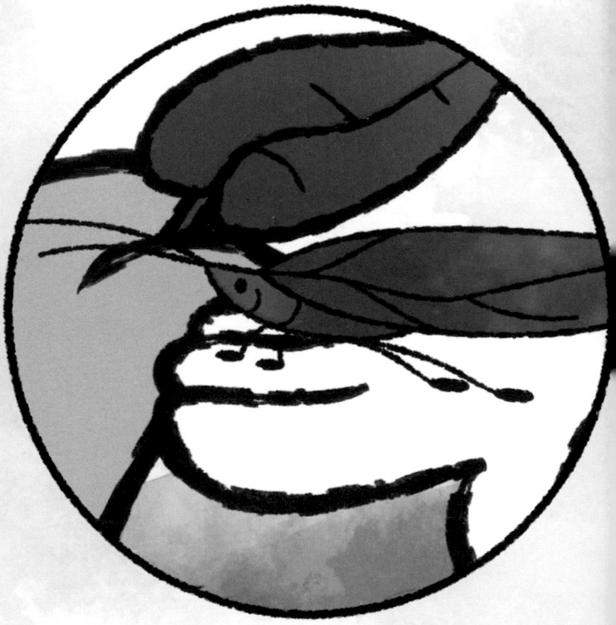

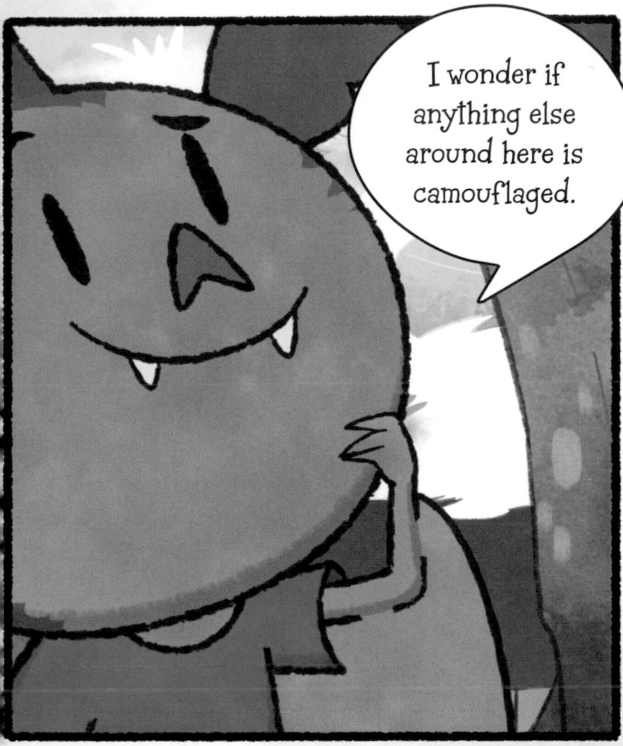
I wonder if anything else around here is camouflaged.

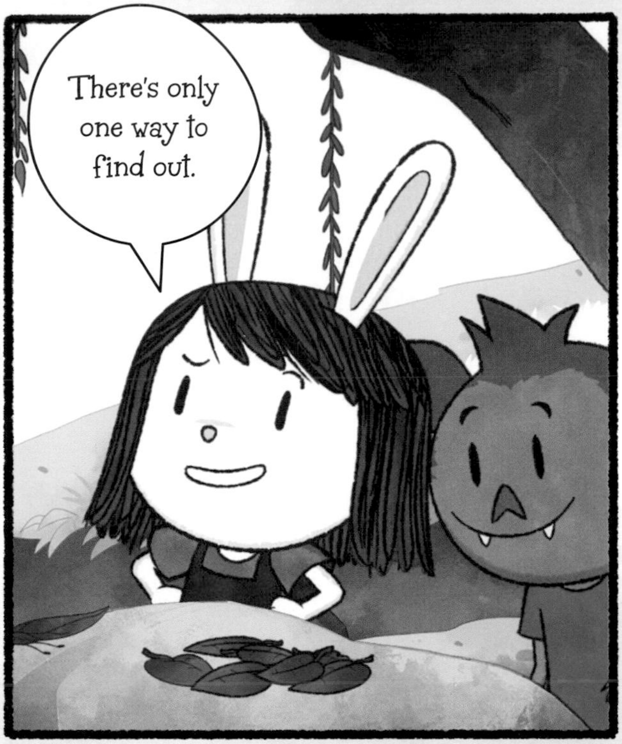
There's only one way to find out.

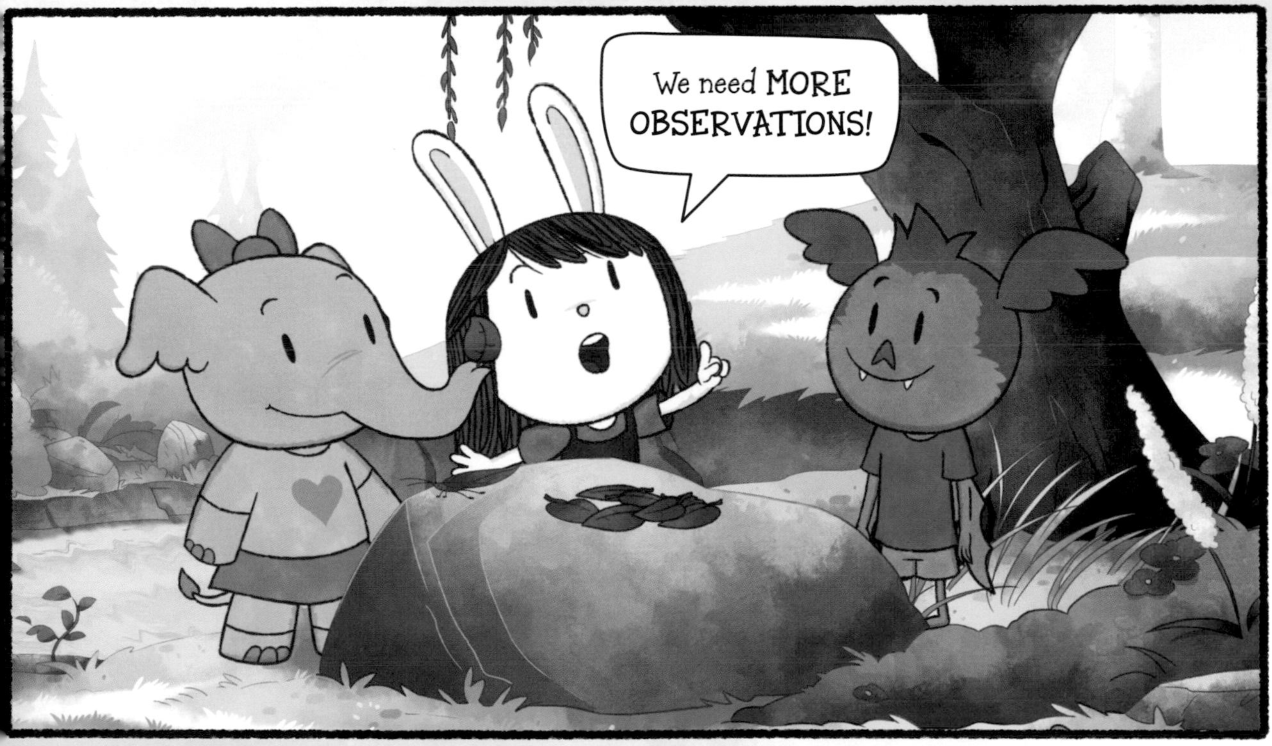
We need MORE OBSERVATIONS!

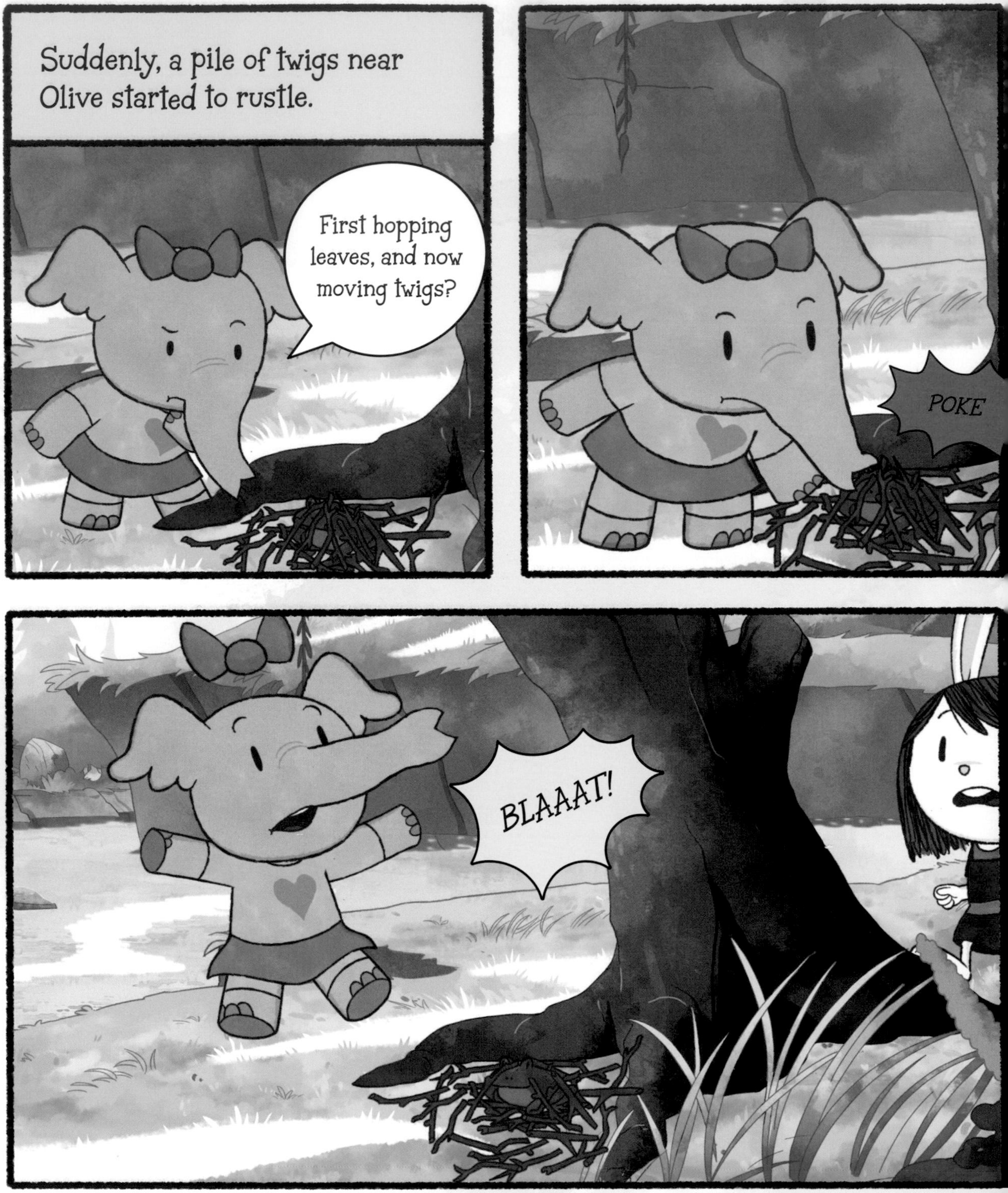
Suddenly, a pile of twigs near Olive started to rustle.
First hopping leaves, and now moving twigs?
POKE
BLAAAT!

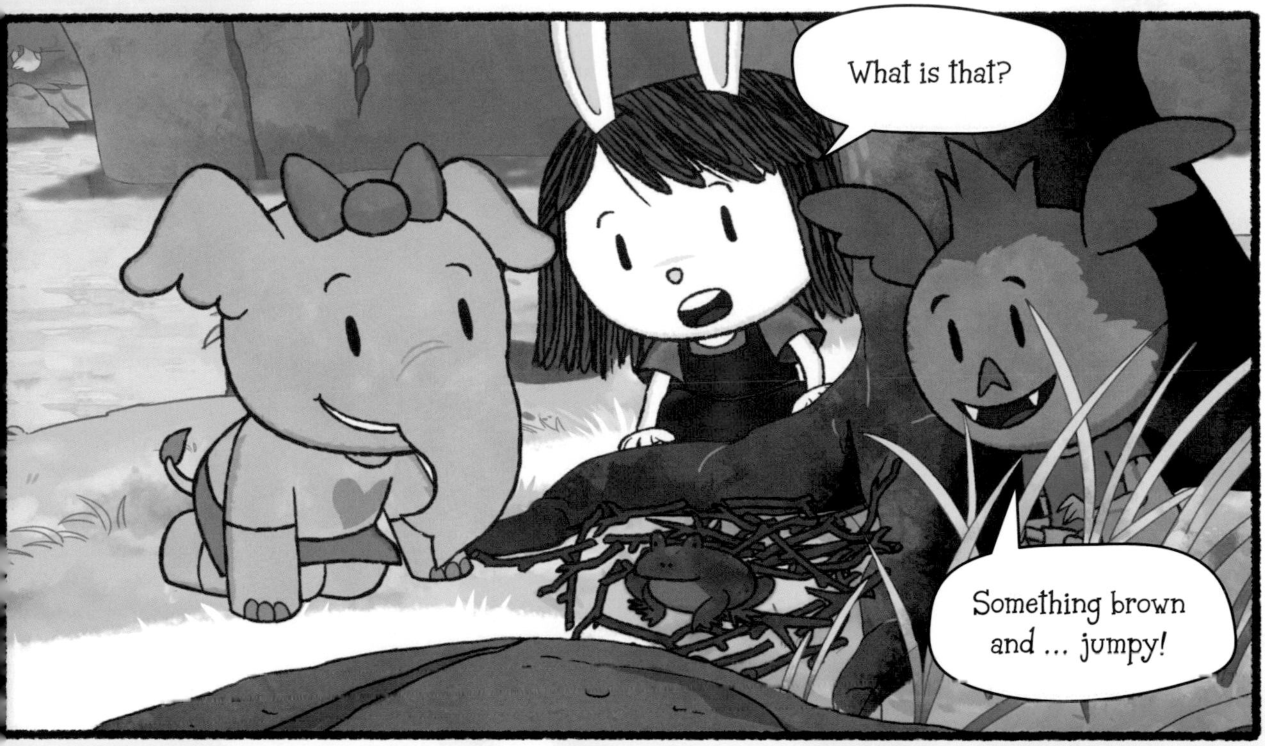
What is that?
Something brown and ... jumpy!

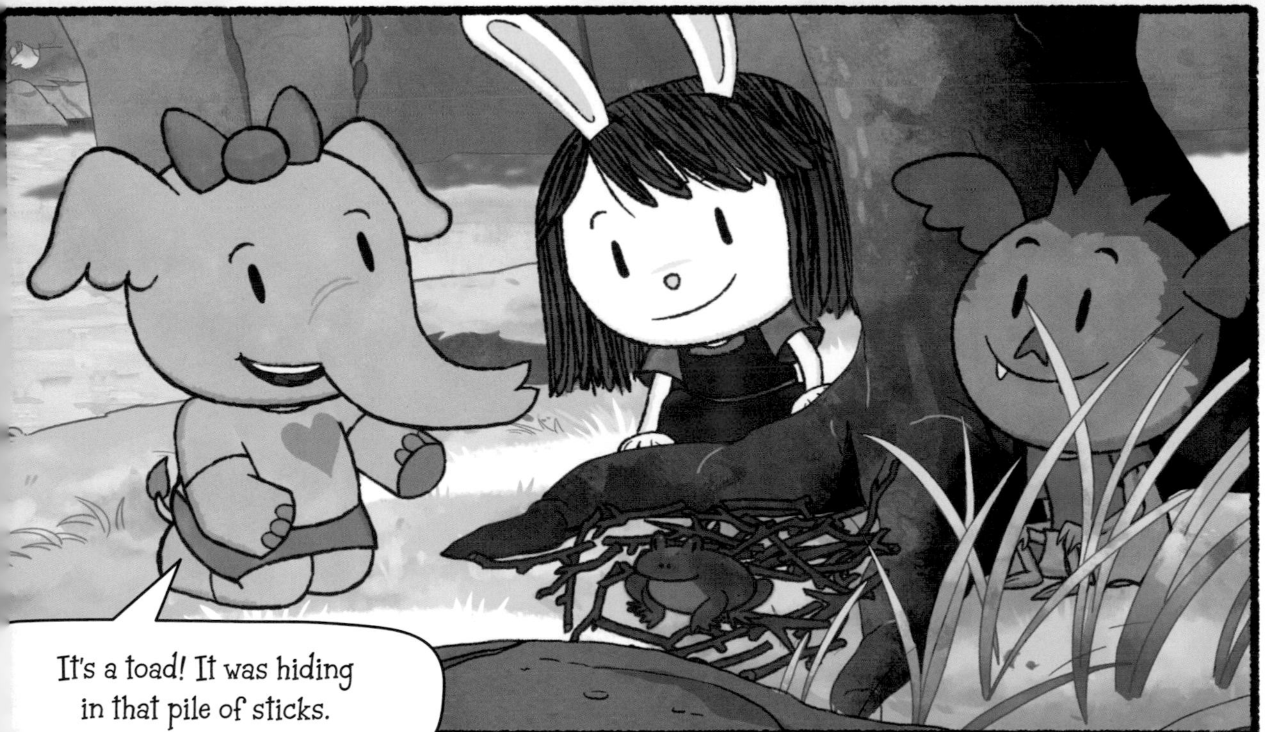
It's a toad! It was hiding in that pile of sticks.

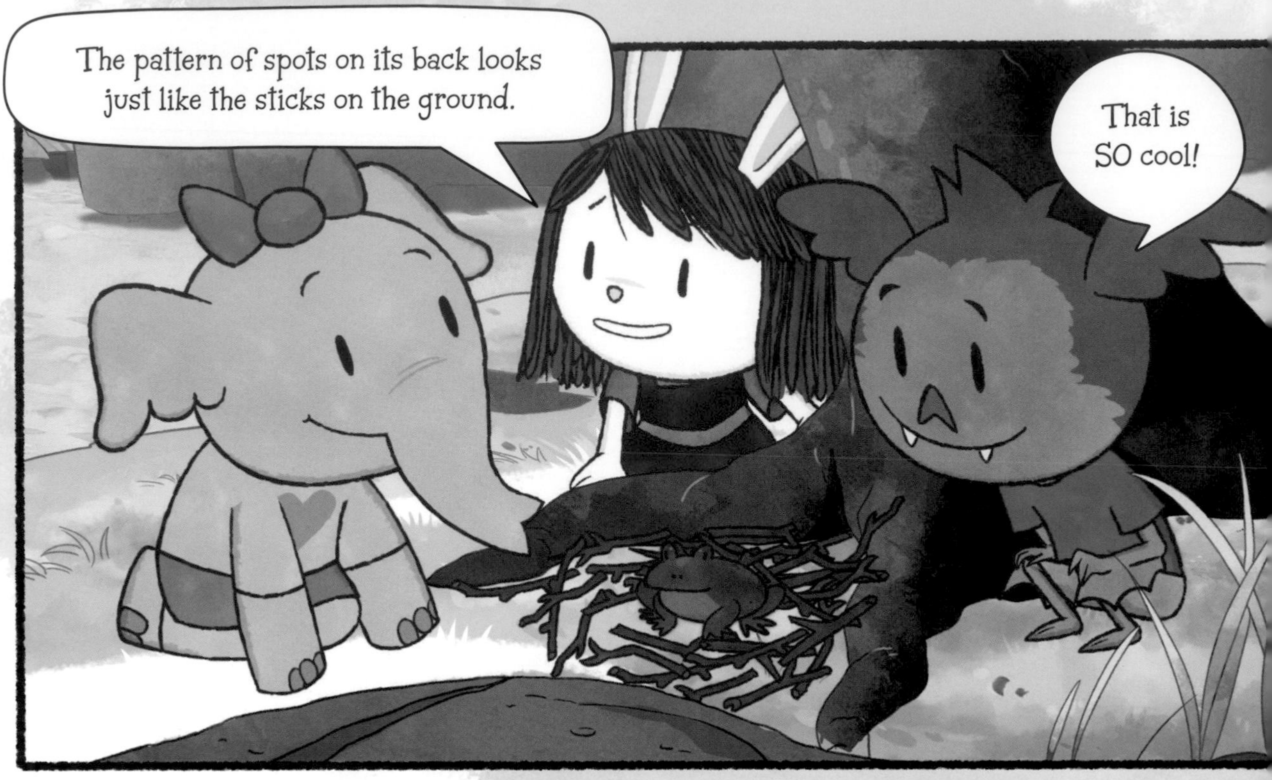
The pattern of spots on its back looks just like the sticks on the ground.
That is SO cool!

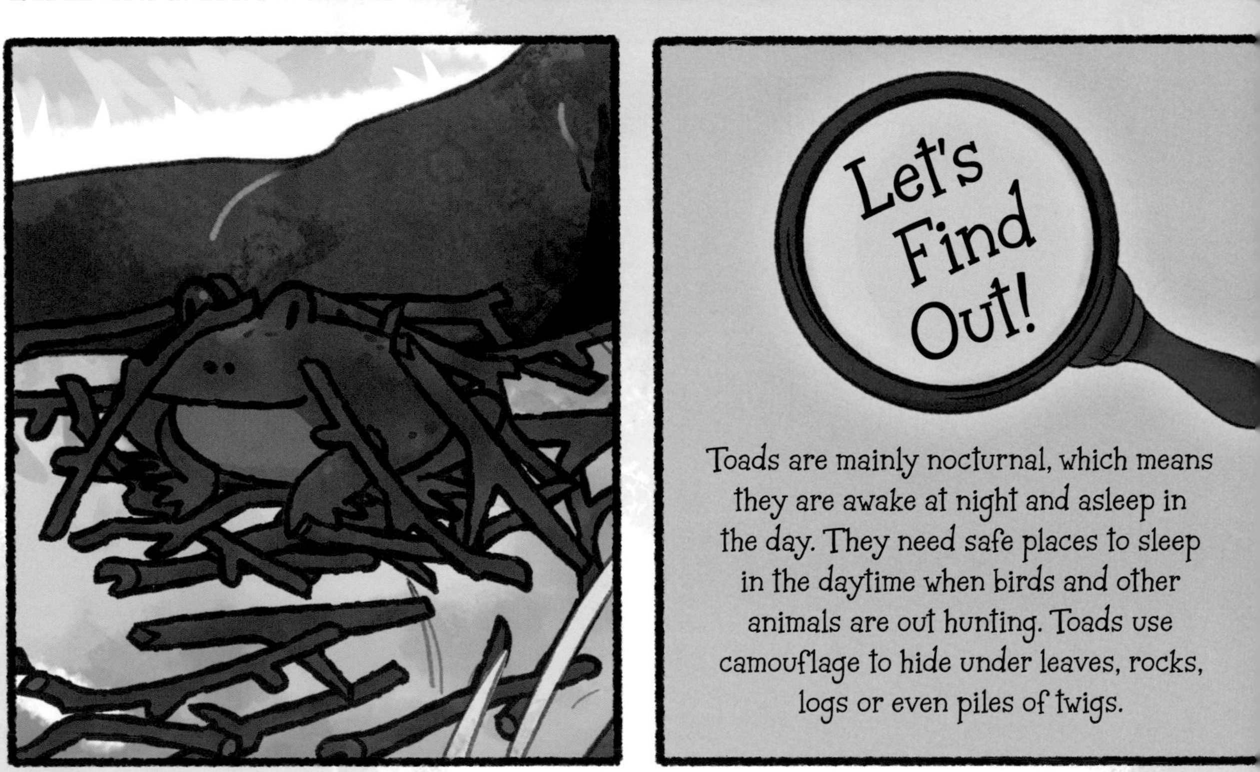

Let's Find Out!

Toads are mainly nocturnal, which means they are awake at night and asleep in the day. They need safe places to sleep in the daytime when birds and other animals are out hunting. Toads use camouflage to hide under leaves, rocks, logs or even piles of twigs.

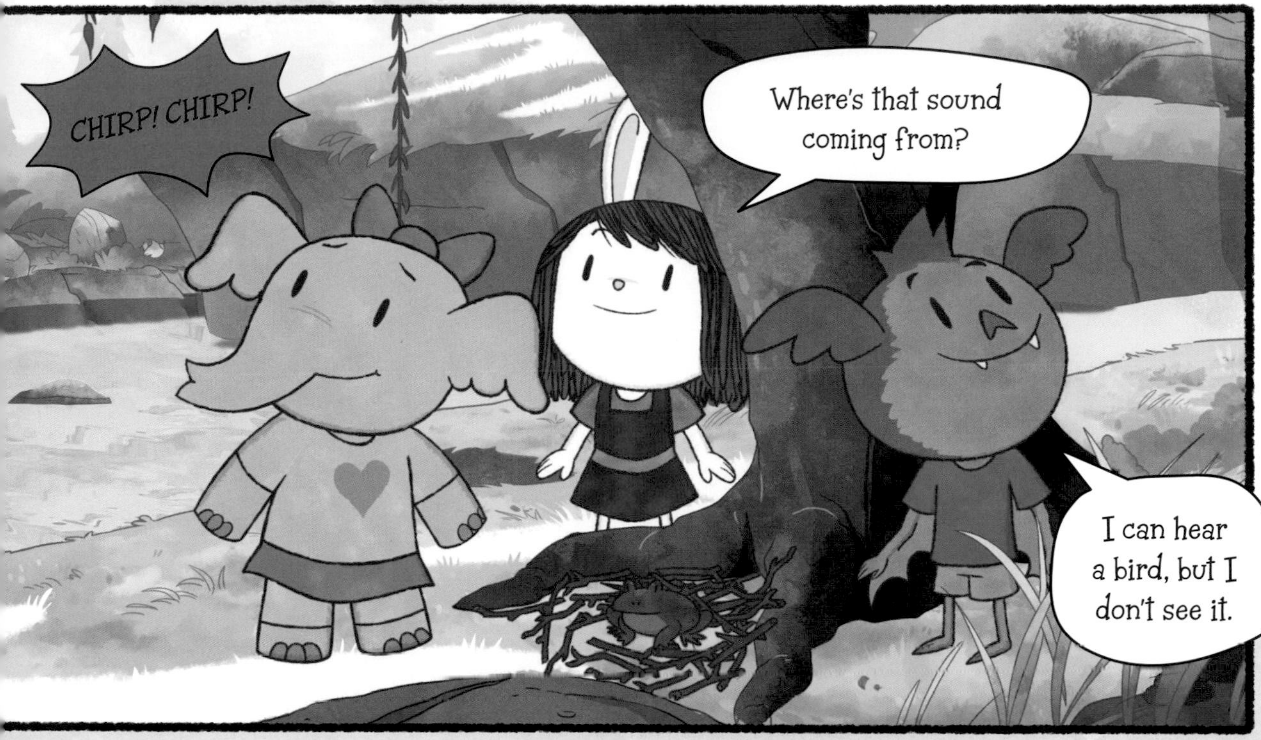
CHIRP! CHIRP!
Where's that sound coming from?
I can hear a bird, but I don't see it.

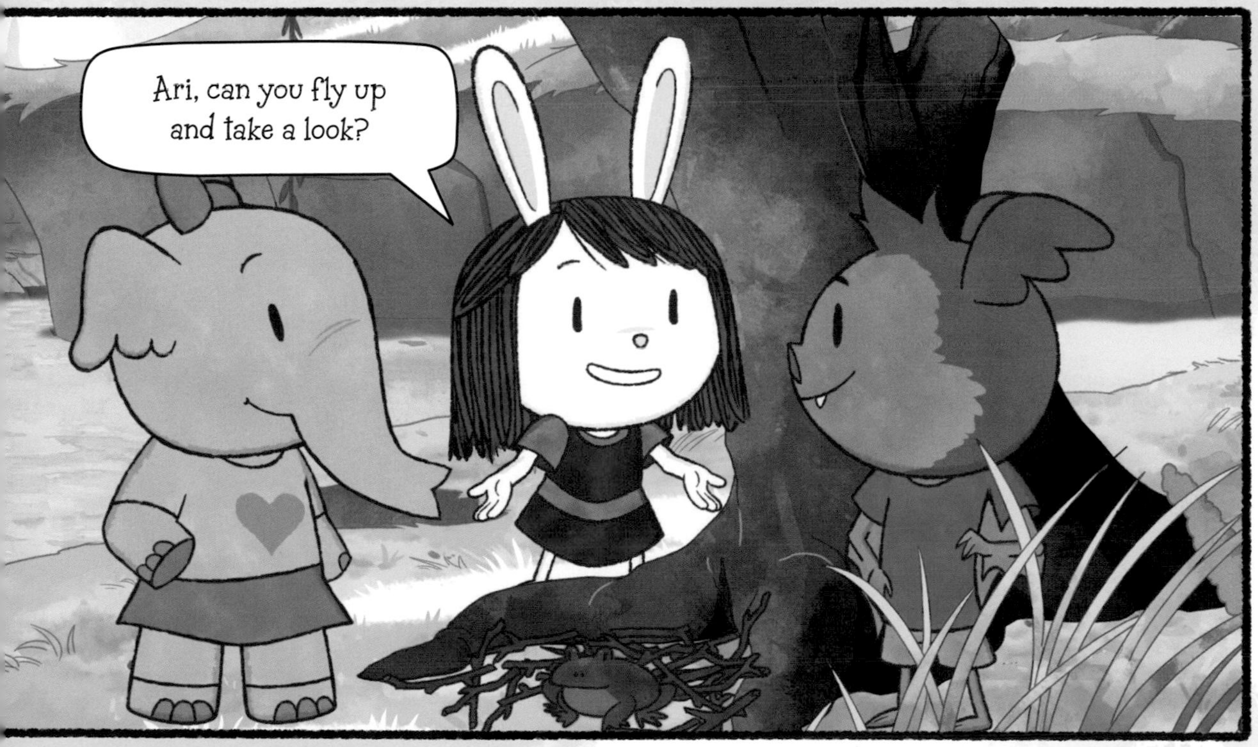
Ari, can you fly up and take a look?

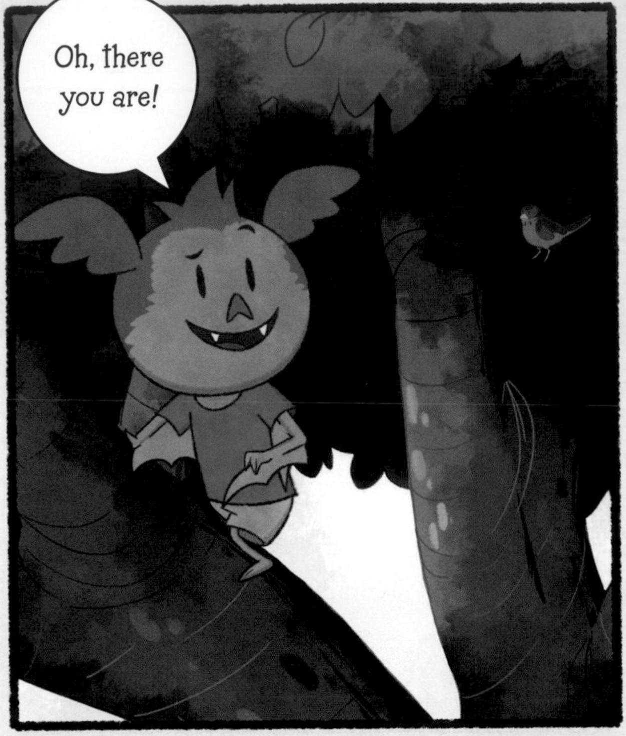
Oh, there you are!

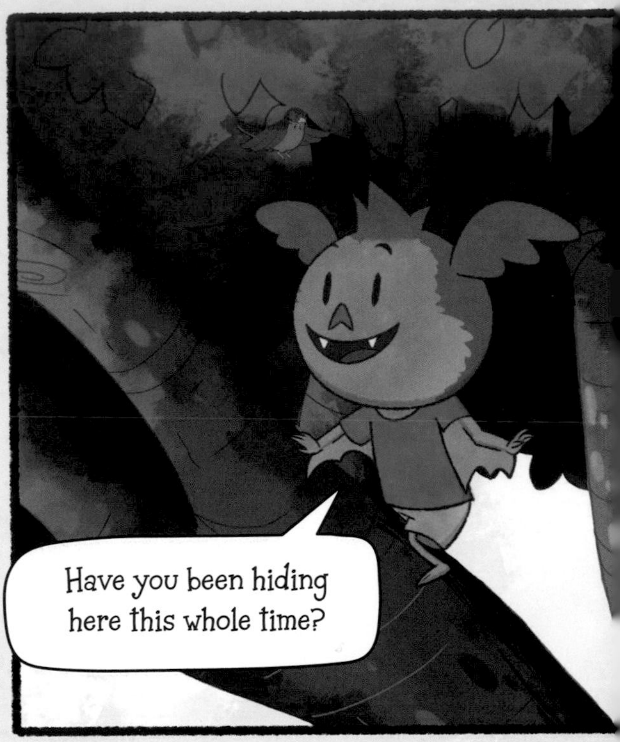
Have you been hiding here this whole time?

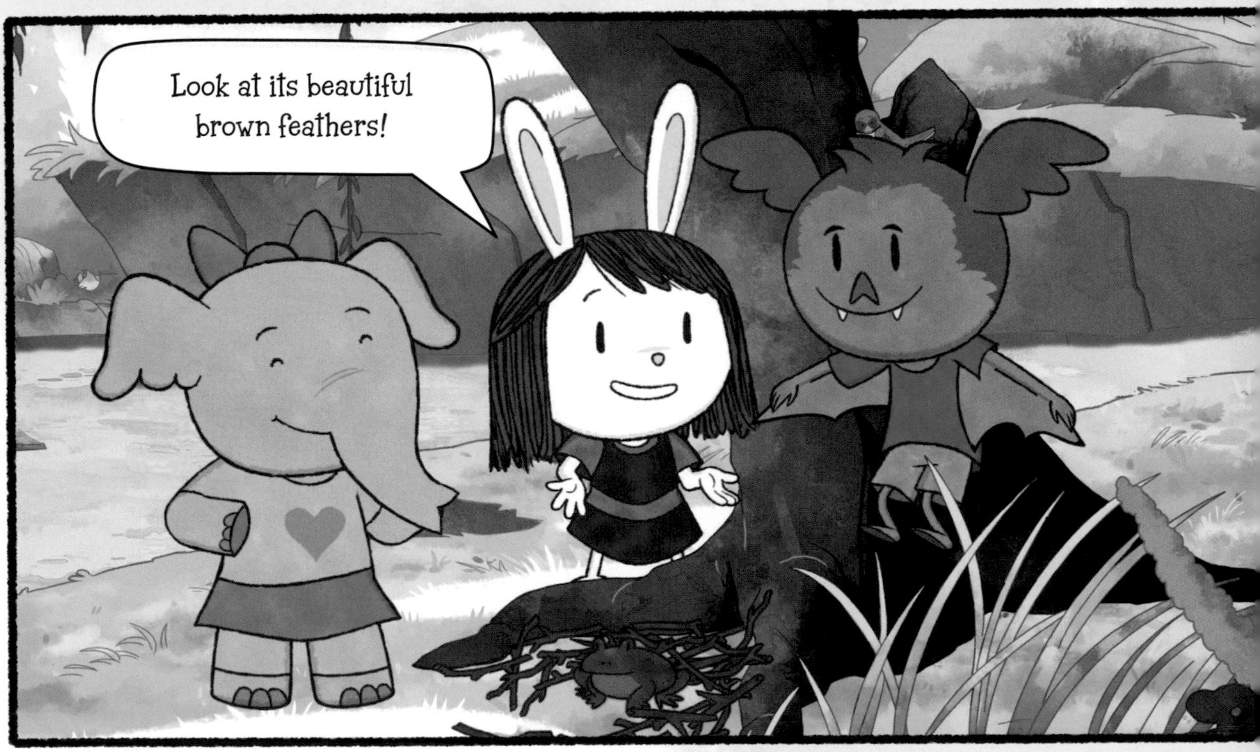
Look at its beautiful brown feathers!

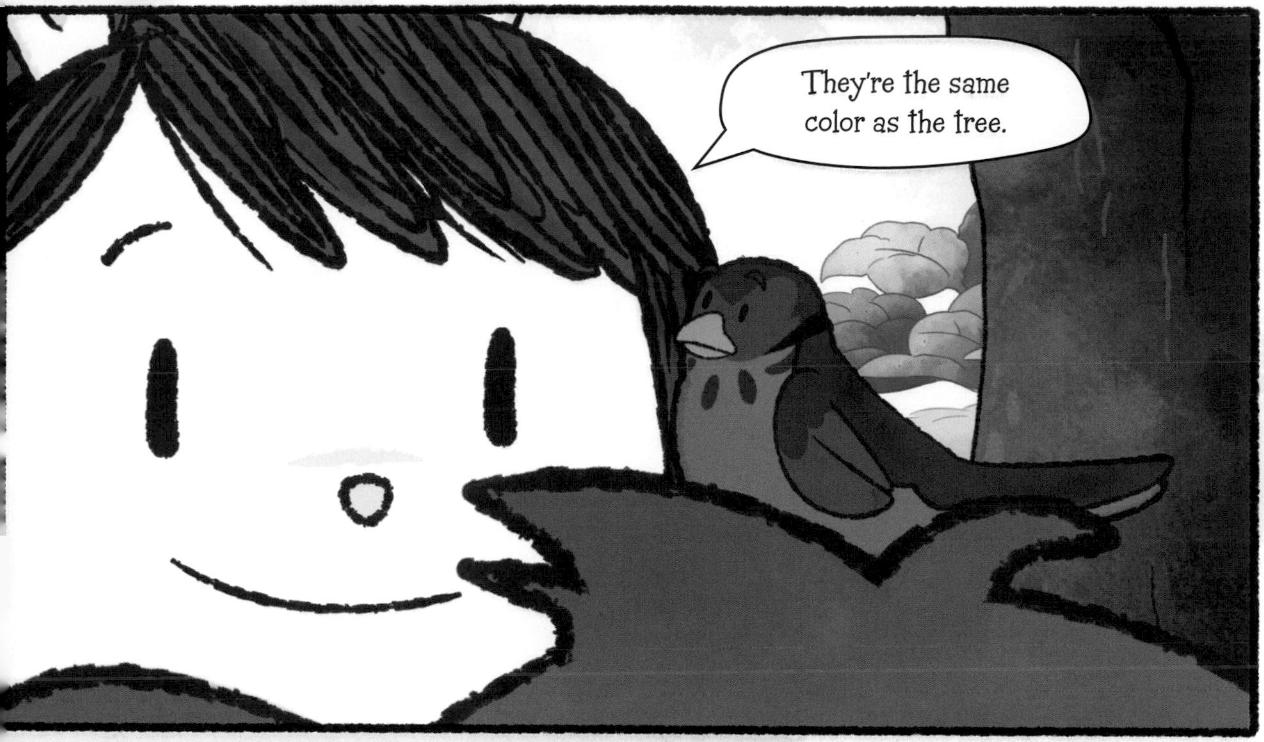
They're the same color as the tree.

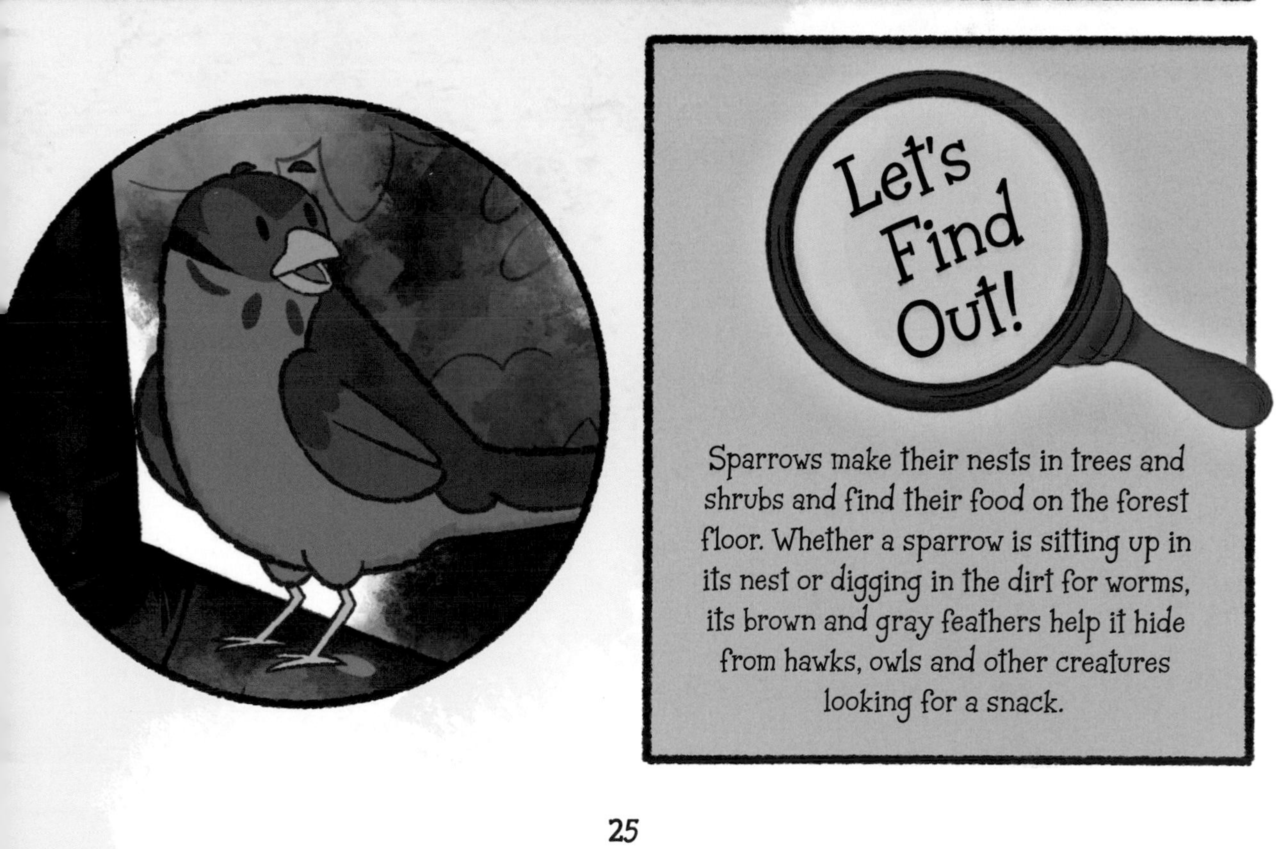

Let's Find Out!

Sparrows make their nests in trees and shrubs and find their food on the forest floor. Whether a sparrow is sitting up in its nest or digging in the dirt for worms, its brown and gray feathers help it hide from hawks, owls and other creatures looking for a snack.

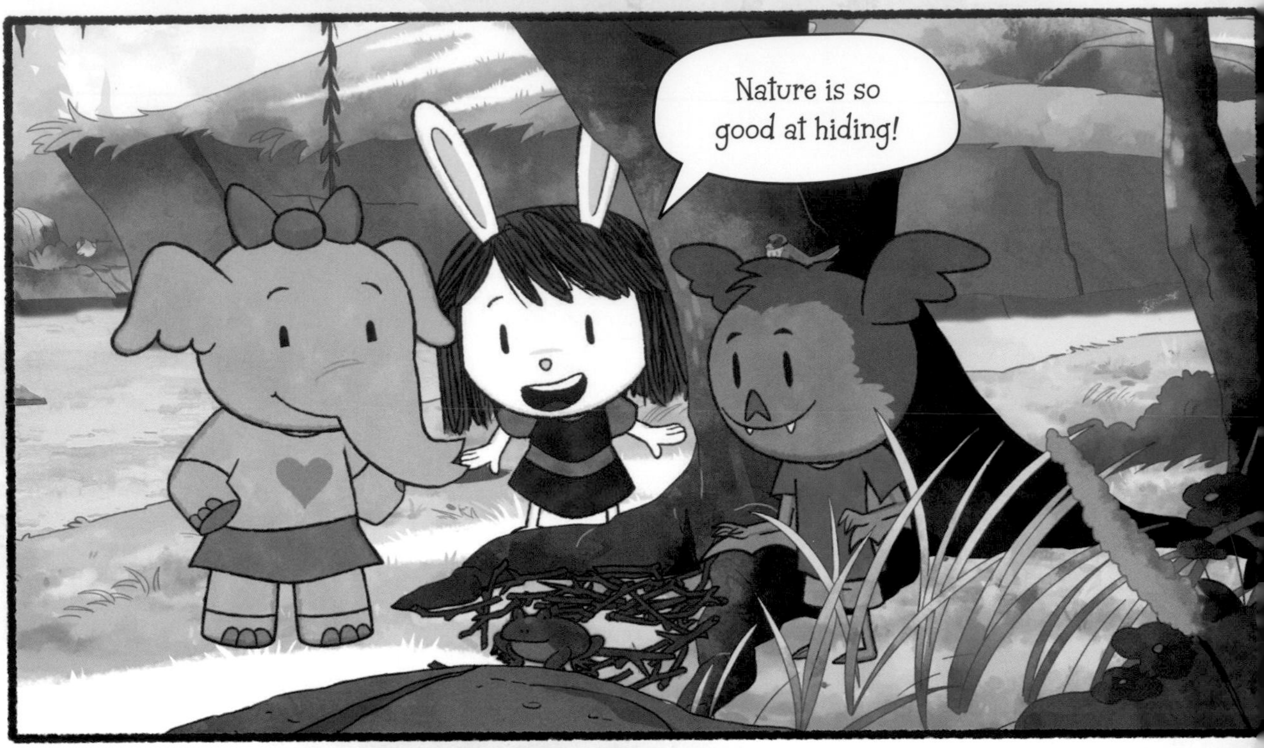
Nature is so good at hiding!

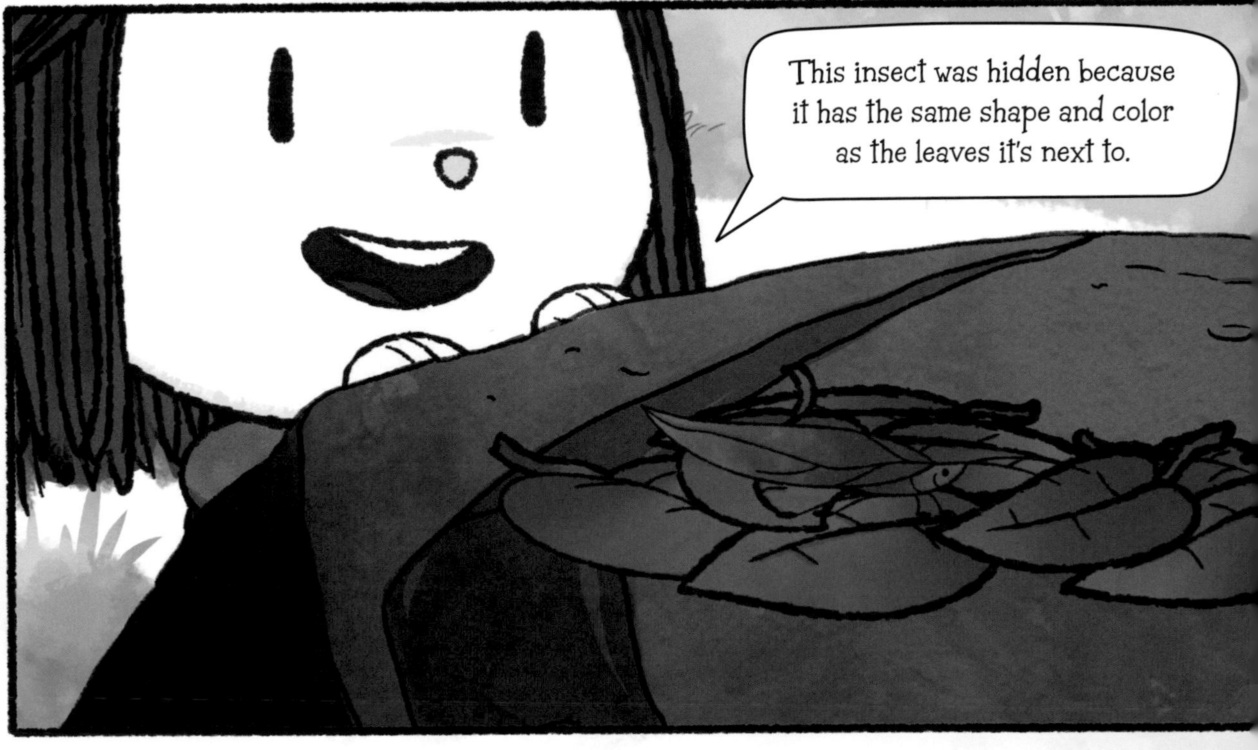
This insect was hidden because it has the same shape and color as the leaves it's next to.

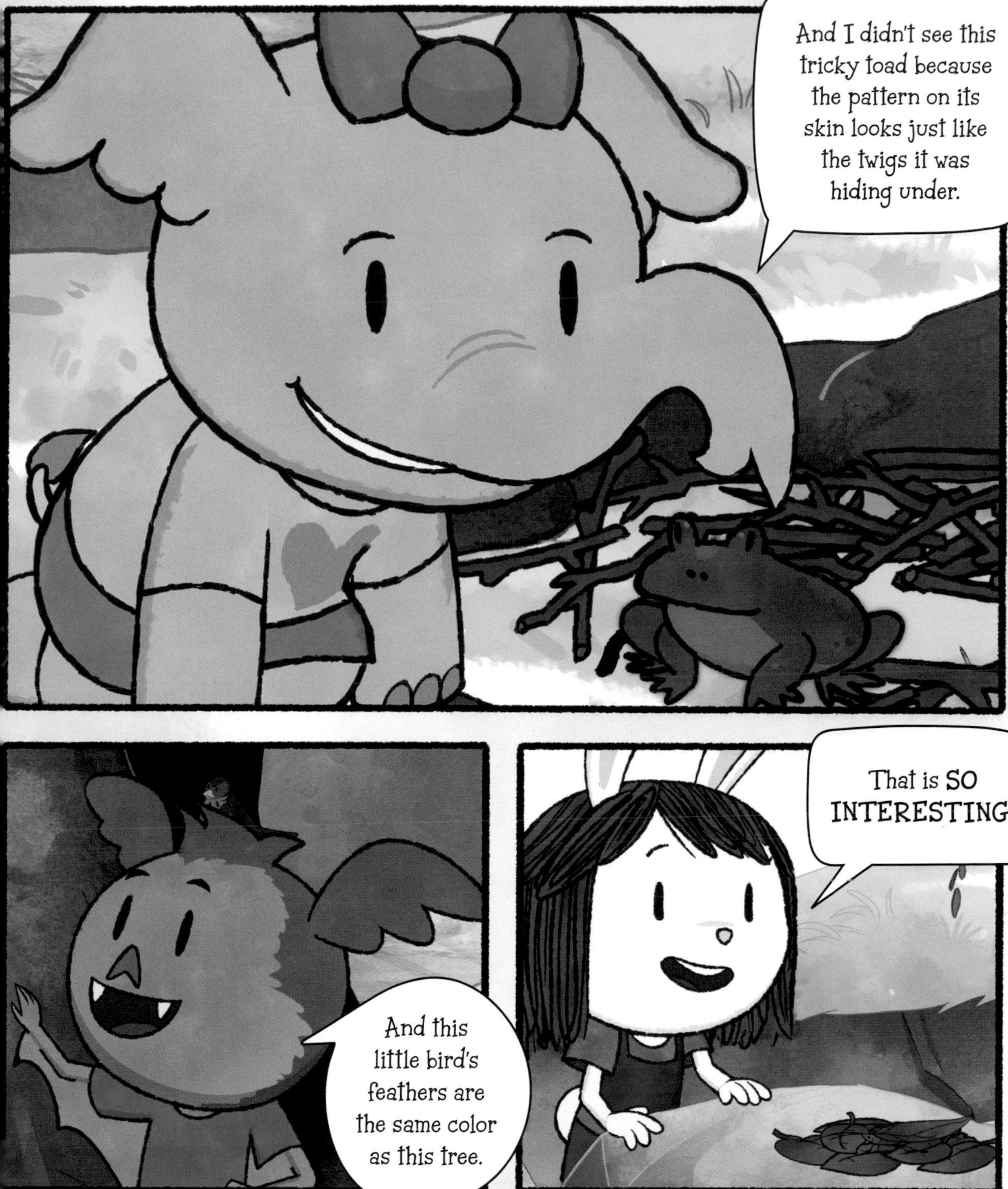
And I didn't see this tricky toad because the pattern on its skin looks just like the twigs it was hiding under.
And this little bird's feathers are the same color as this tree.
That is SO INTERESTING!

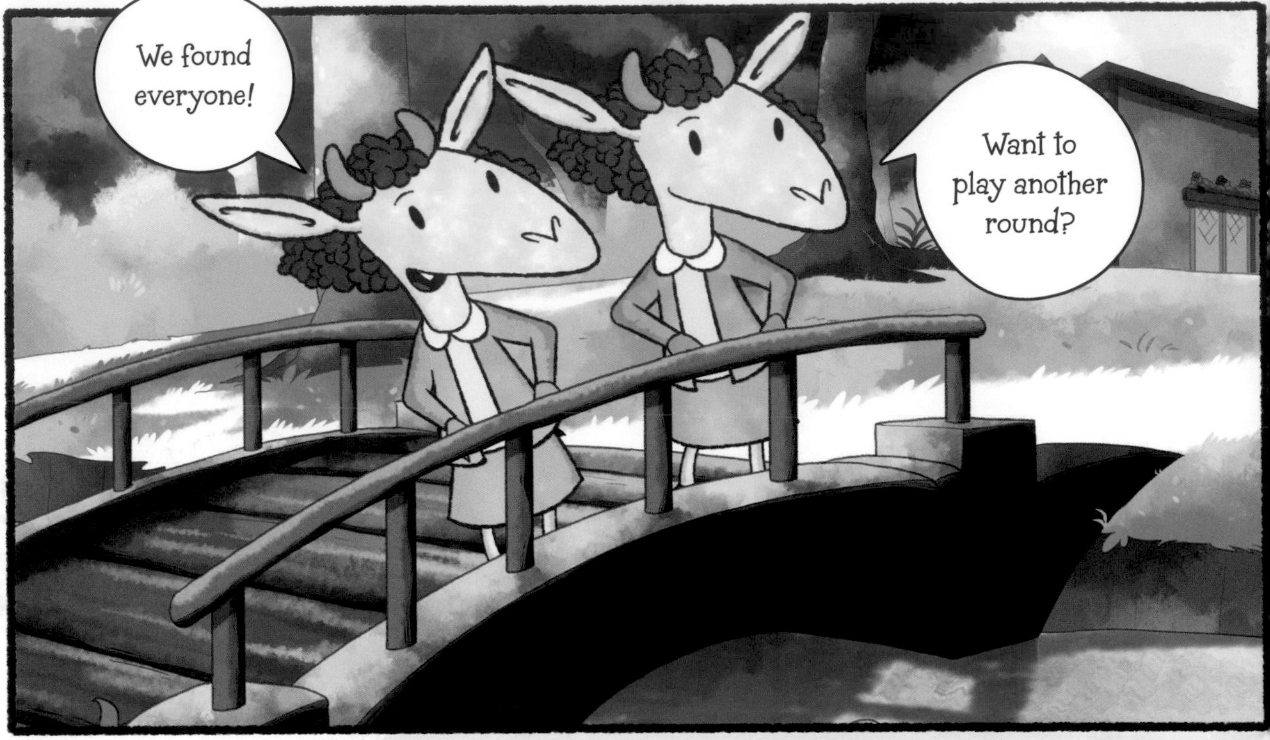
We found everyone!
Want to play another round?

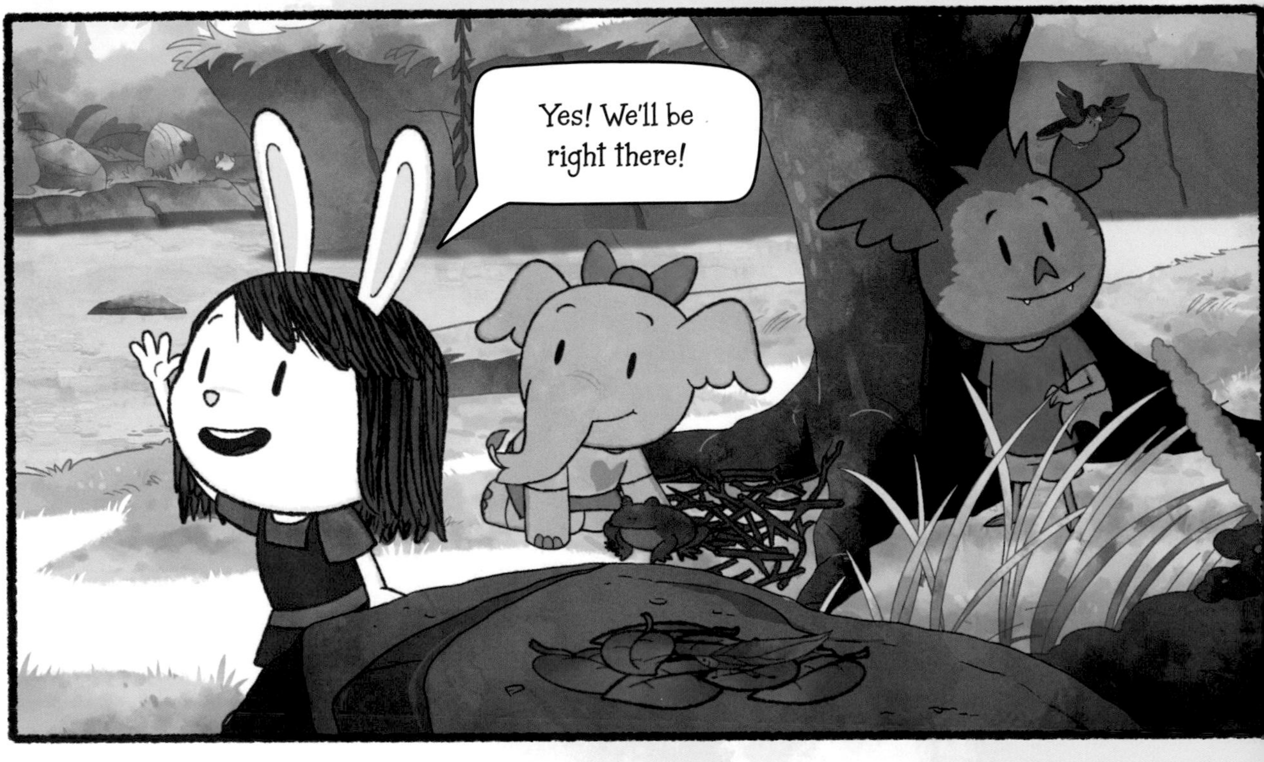
Yes! We'll be right there!

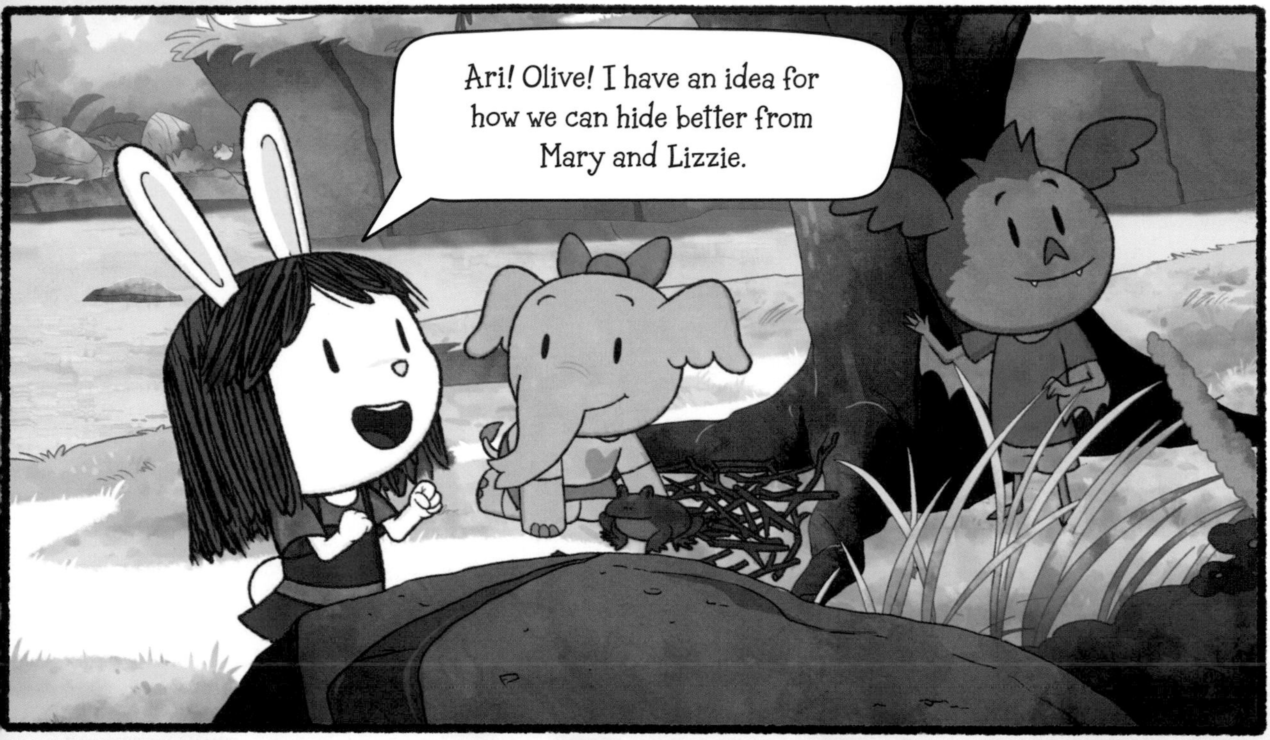
Ari! Olive! I have an idea for how we can hide better from Mary and Lizzie.

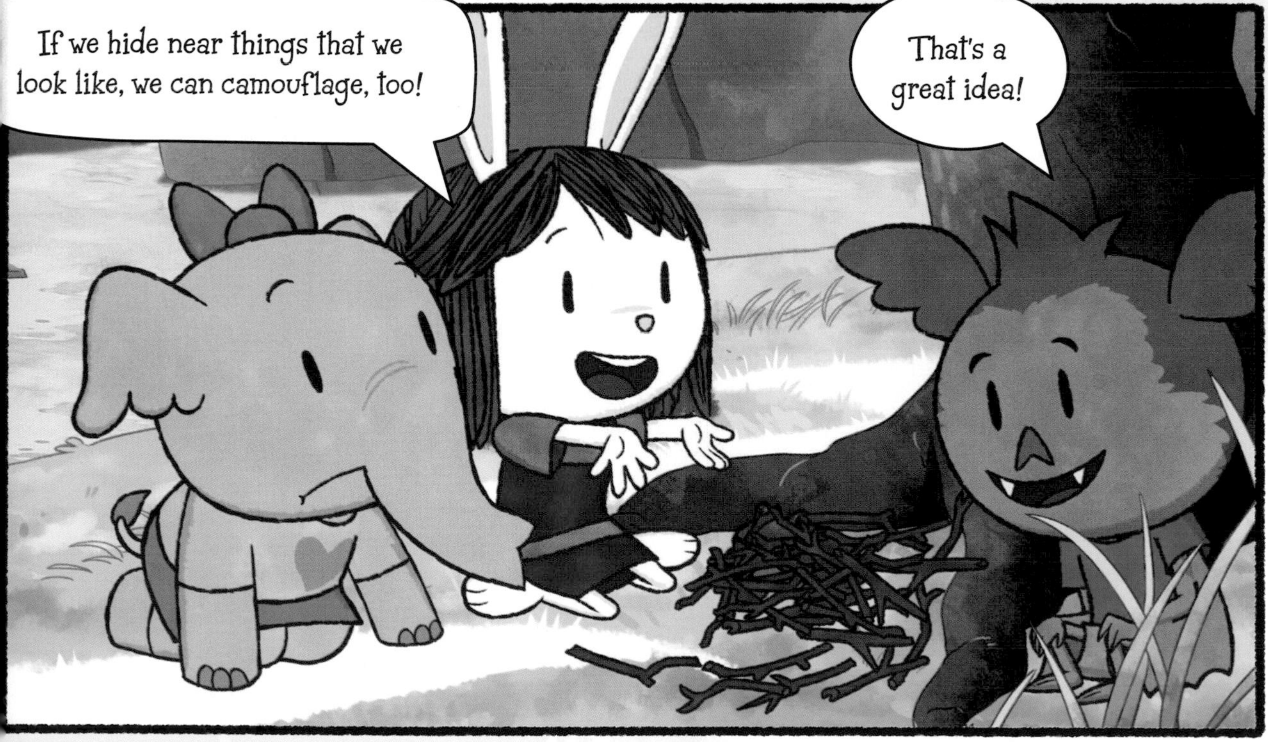
If we hide near things that we look like, we can camouflage, too!
That's a great idea!

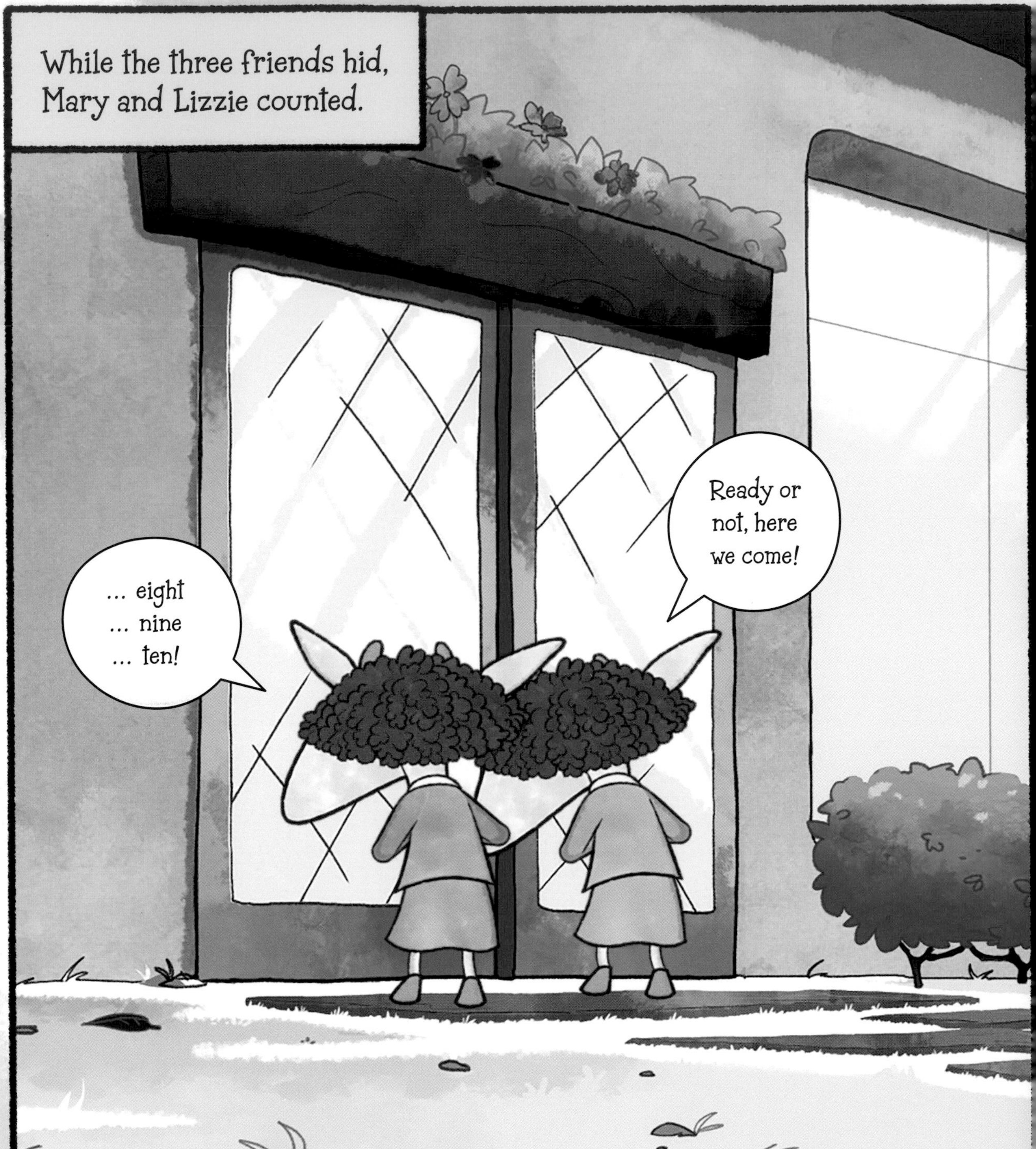
While the three friends hid,
Mary and Lizzie counted.
... eight ... nine ... ten!
Ready or not, here we come!

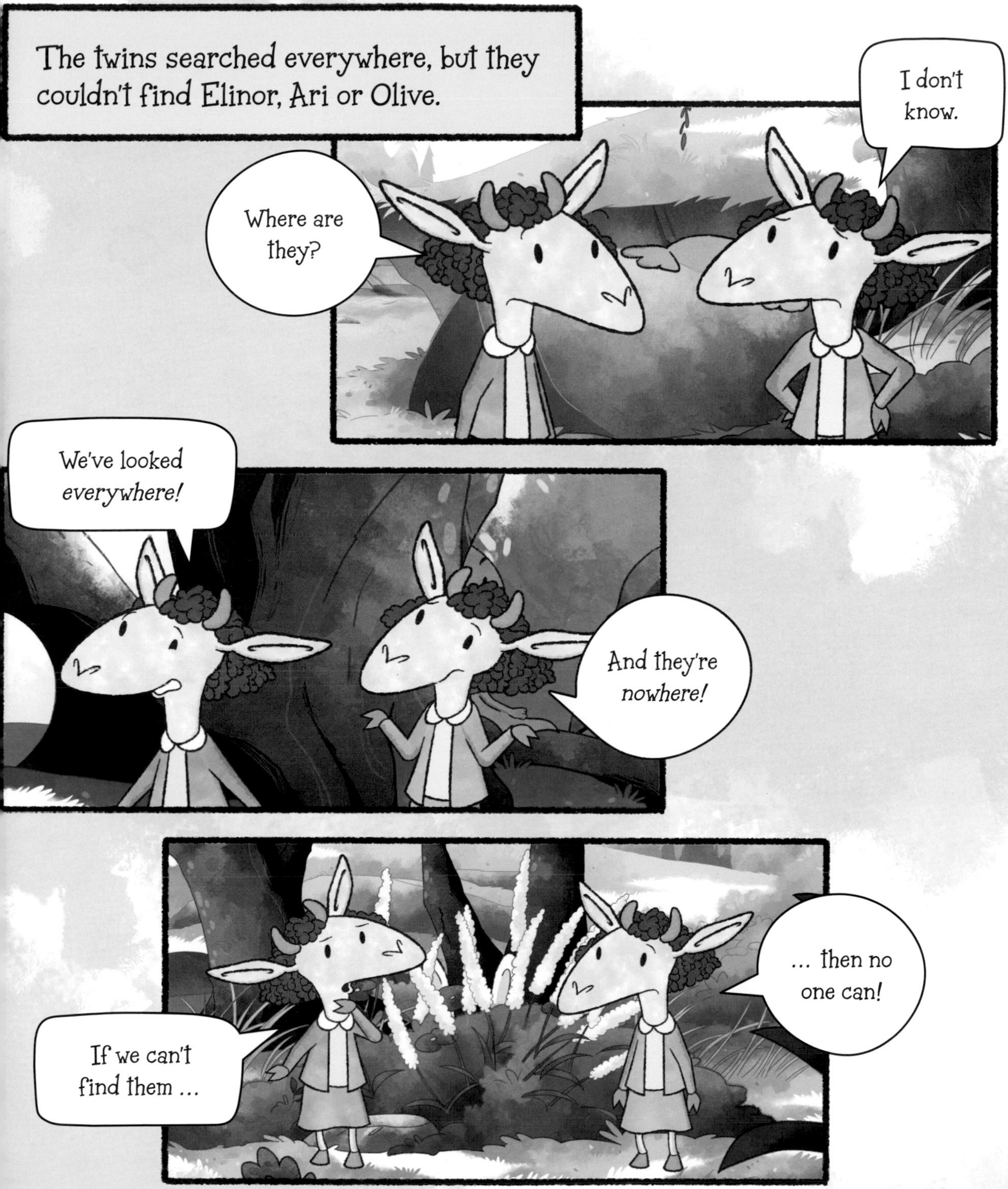
The twins searched everywhere, but they couldn't find Elinor, Ari or Olive.
Where are they?
I don't know.
We've looked *everywhere!*
And they're *nowhere!*
If we can't find them ...
... then no one can!

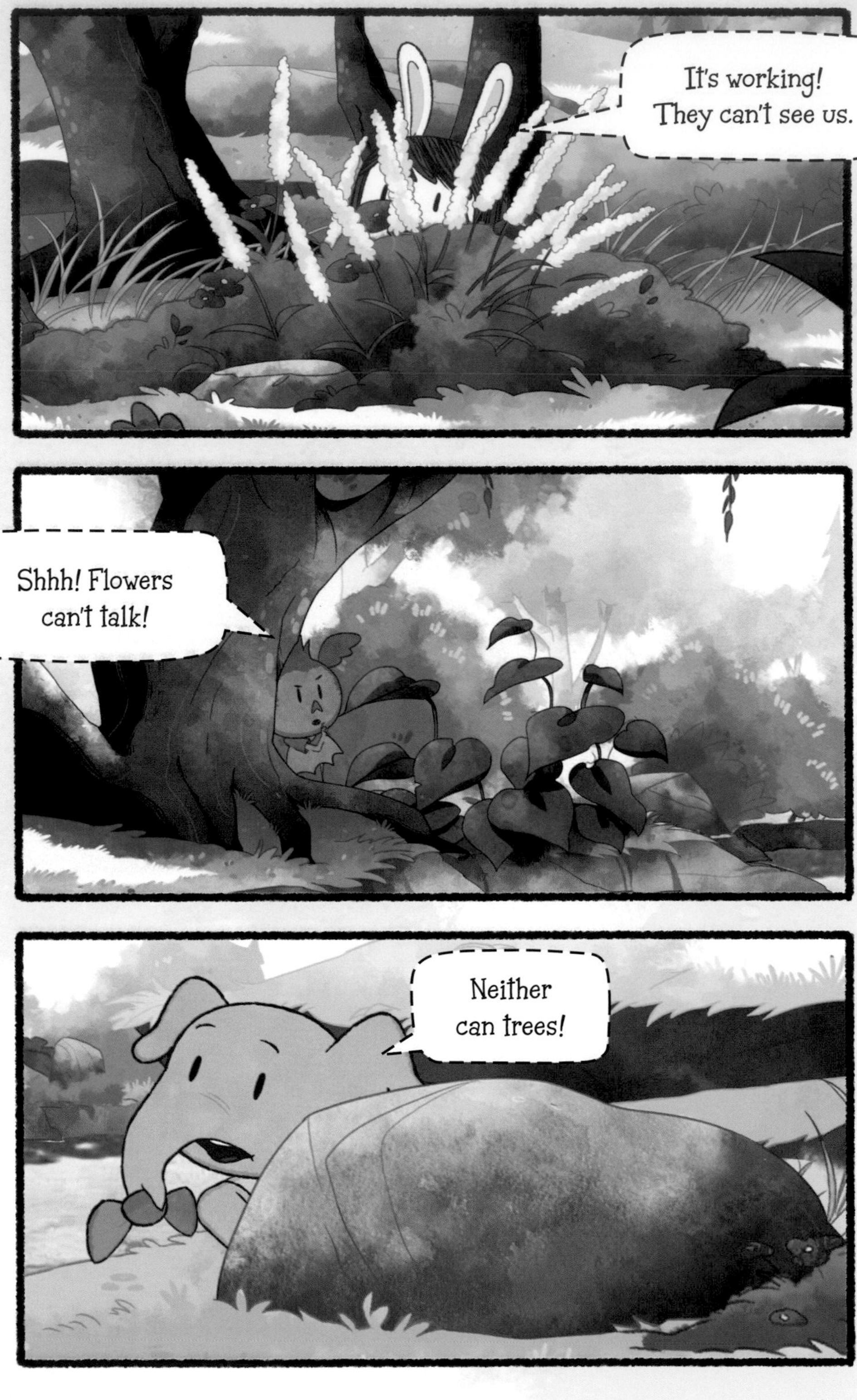
It's working! They can't see us.
Shhh! Flowers can't talk!
Neither can trees!

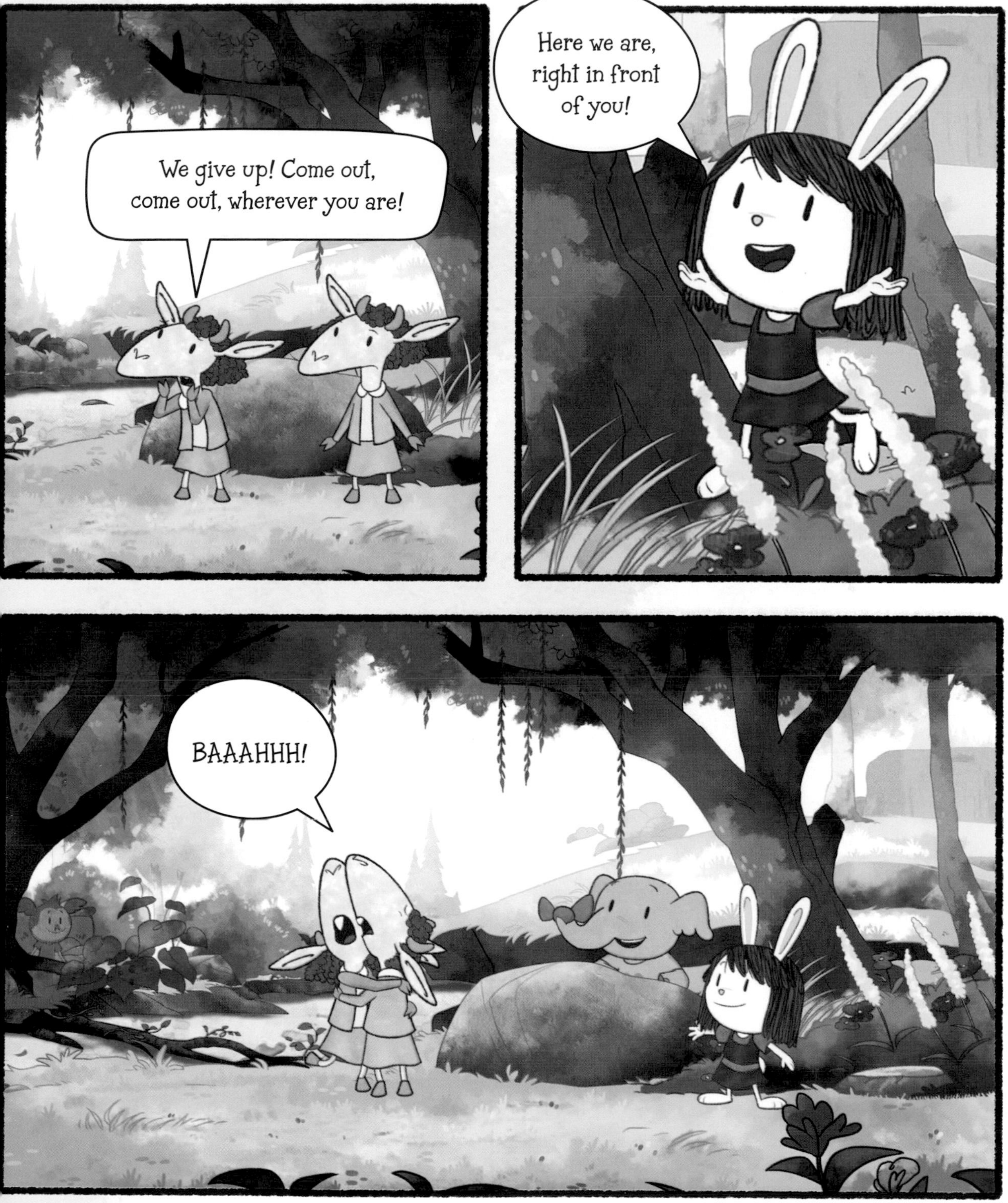
We give up! Come out, come out, wherever you are!
Here we are, right in front of you!
BAAAHHH!

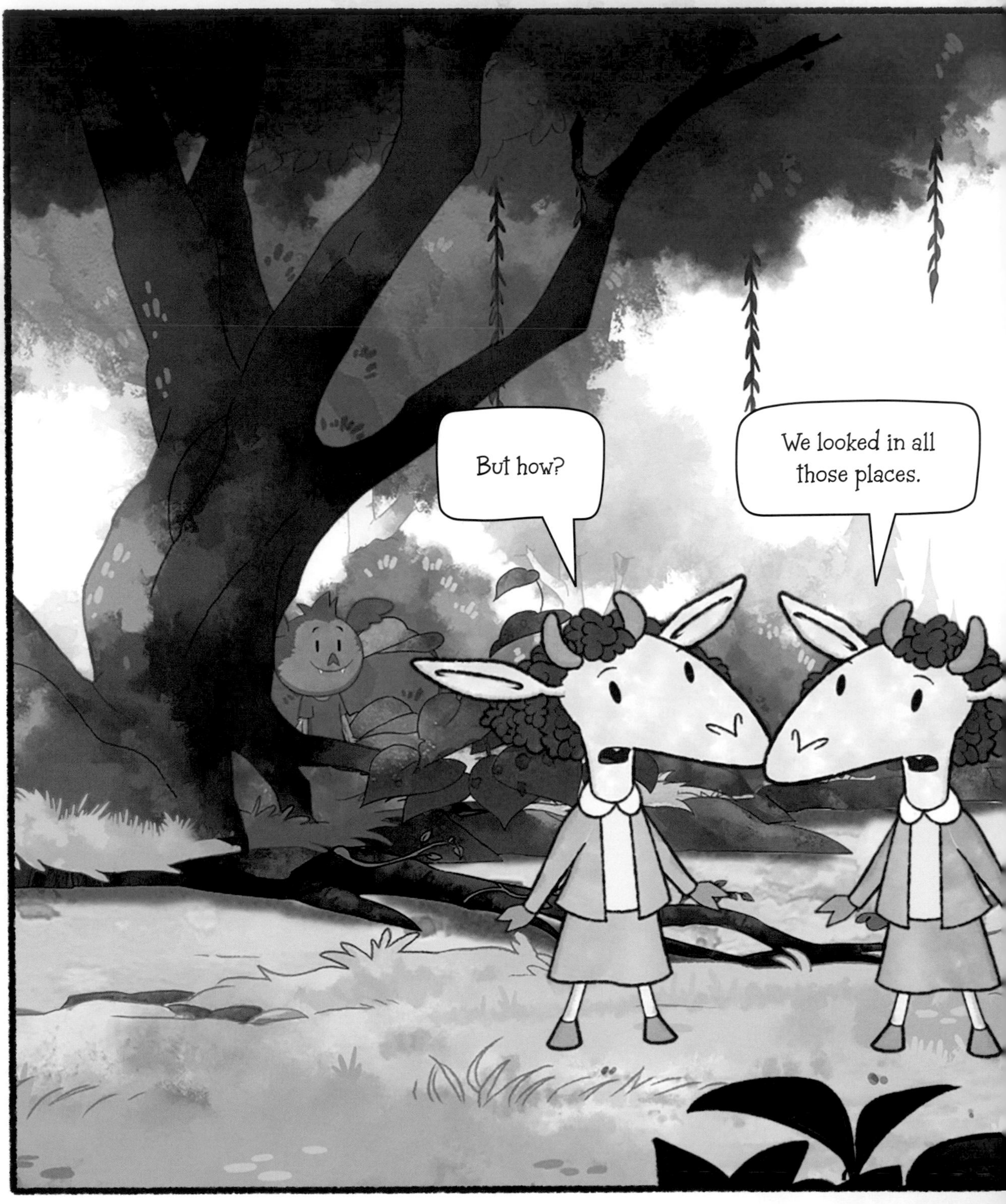
But how?
We looked in all those places.

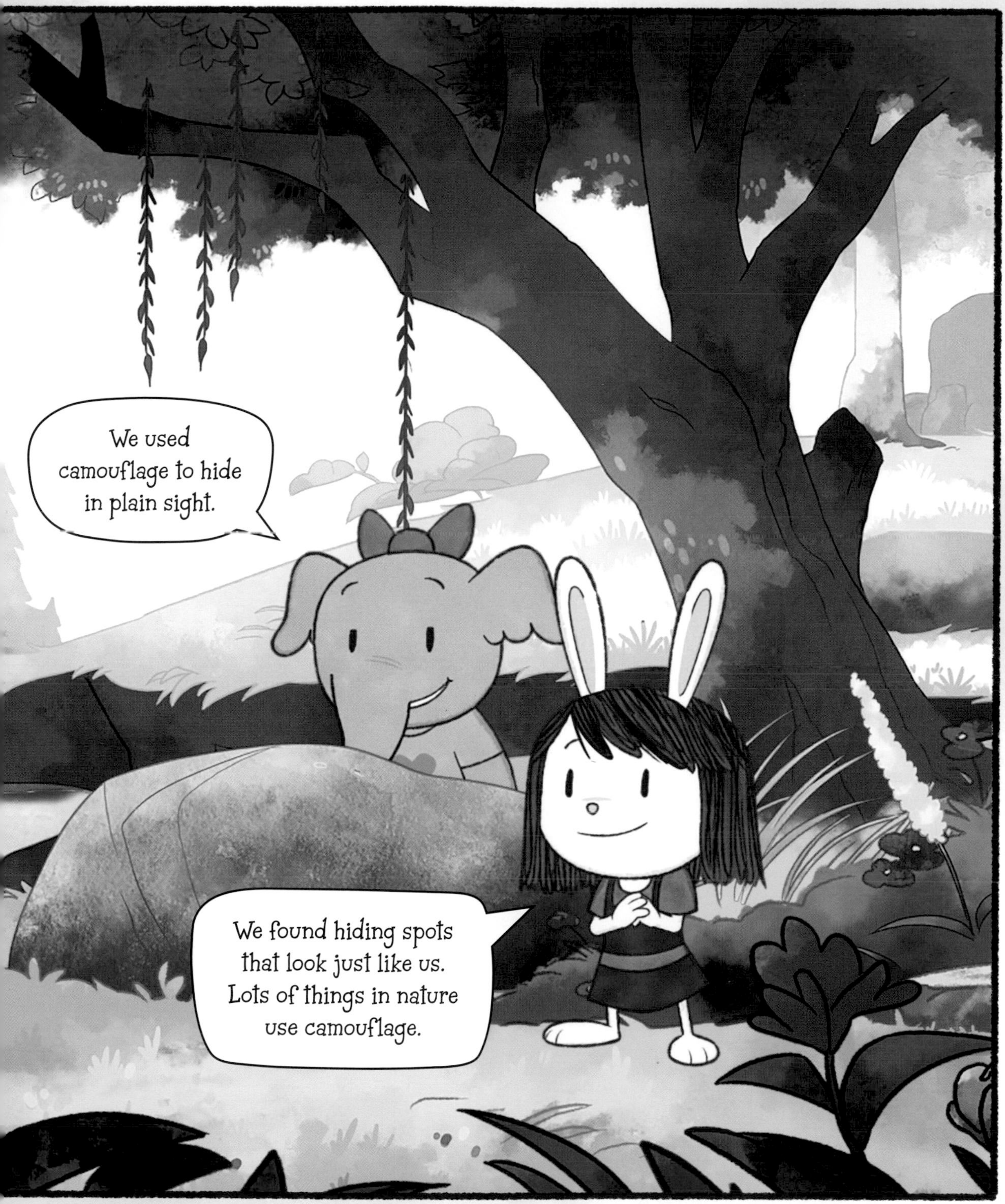
We used camouflage to hide in plain sight.
We found hiding spots that look just like us. Lots of things in nature use camouflage.

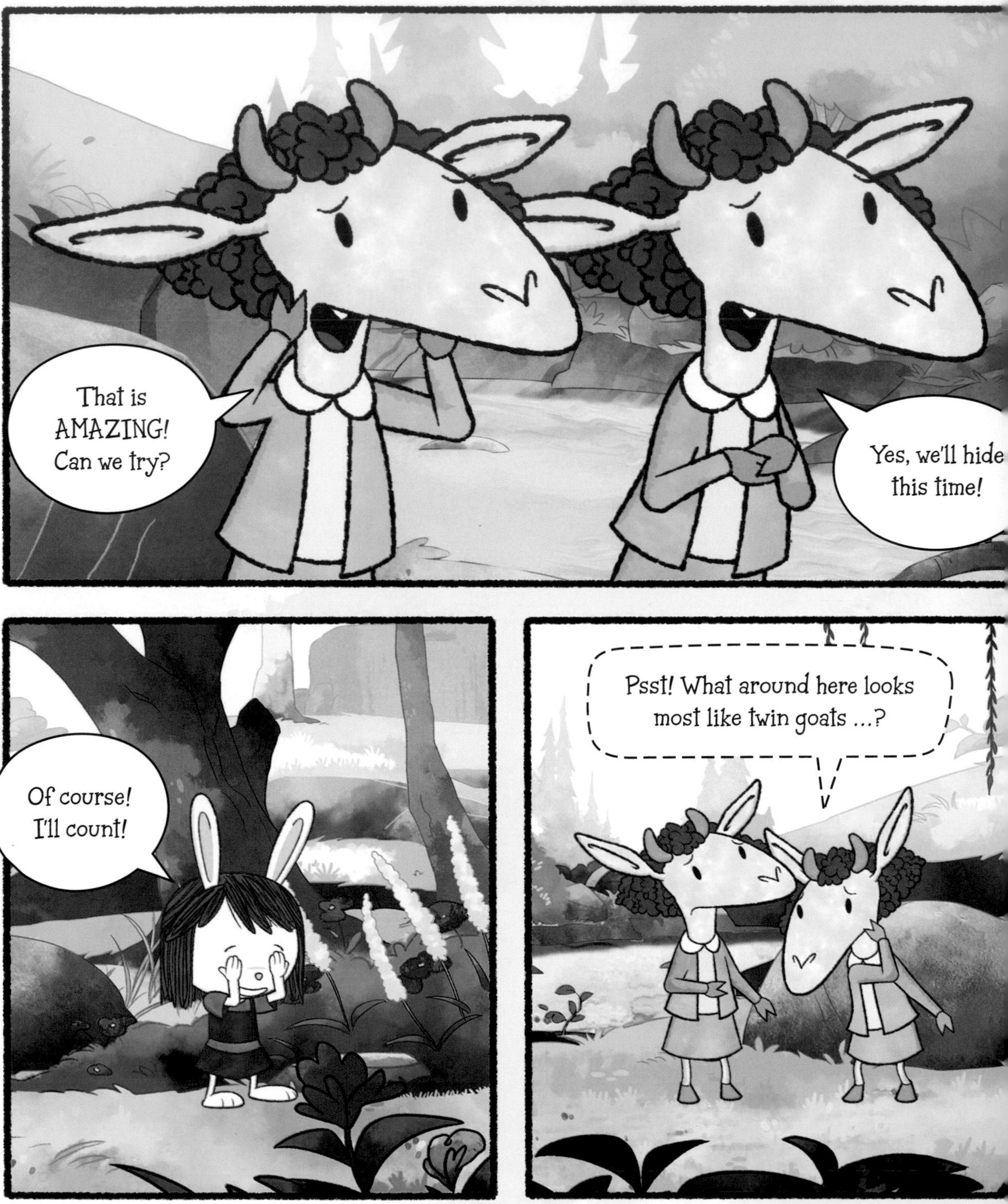
That is AMAZING! Can we try?
Yes, we'll hide this time!
Of course! I'll count!
Psst! What around here looks most like twin goats ...?

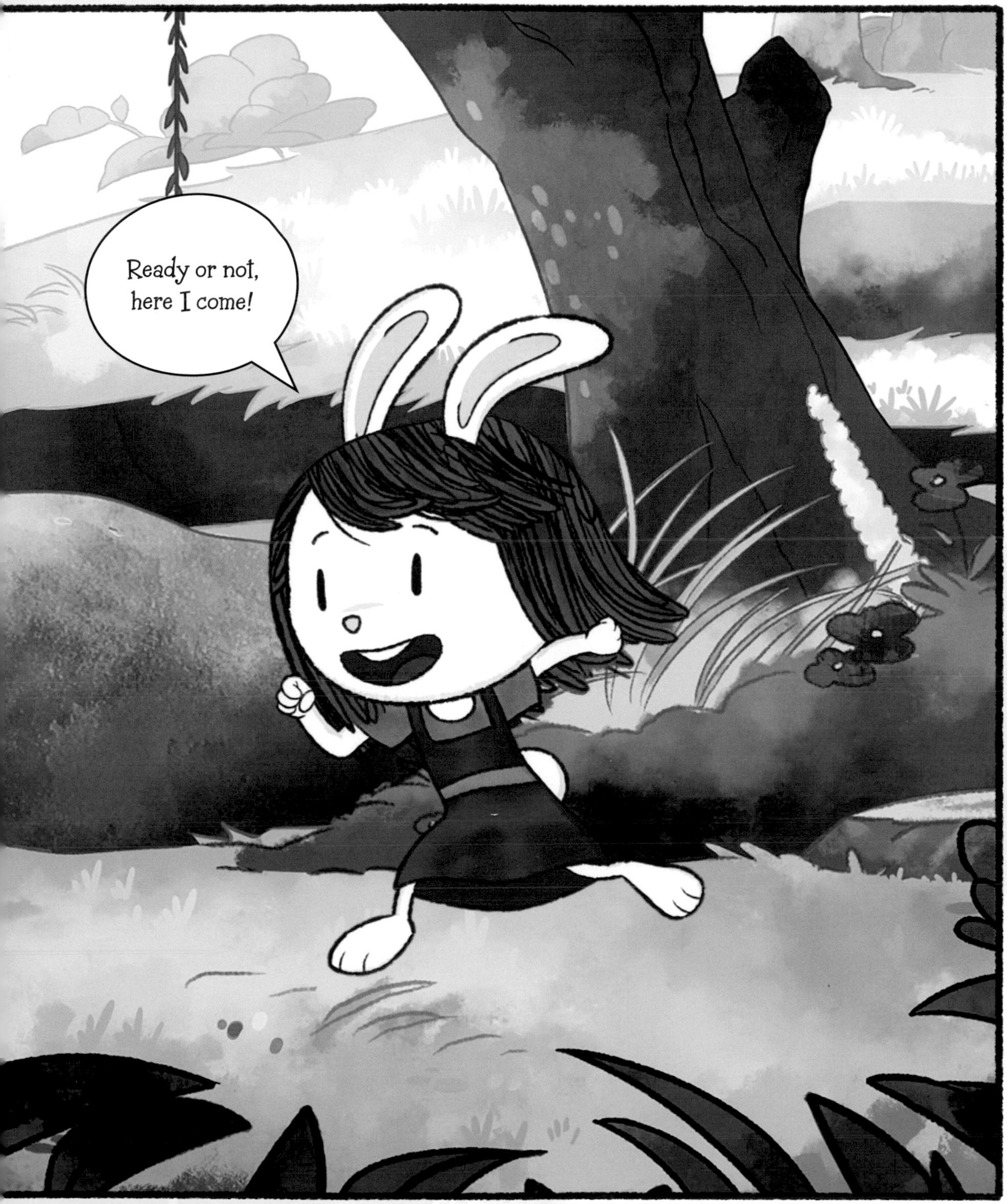
Ready or not, here I come!

Hide-and-Seek in Nature

The world around us is full of life, even if we don't always see it at first. In this activity, you will visit a park and play hide-and-seek with the creatures around you.

You'll need:

- ❡ a notebook
- ❡ a pencil or crayons
- ❡ an assistant (a grown-up)

You could also bring any of these observation tools:

- ❡ a camera
- ❡ binoculars
- ❡ a magnifying glass

Let's Experiment!

1. Head to a nearby park with your assistant. If you have any of the observation tools from the list above, bring them with you.

2. Take a quick look all around you. Do you see any animals right away? Maybe you see a dog out for a walk with its owner, or a squirrel sitting on the branch of a tree.

3. Write down or draw the creatures you can see easily.

4. Now look closer. Crouch down and observe a flower petal or a blade of grass. Get up close to look at the bark of a tree or the soil.

Listen closely, too. Can you hear a bird singing? Or a cricket chirping? If you have binoculars or a magnifying glass, use them to help you look all around.

5. Write down or draw the creatures you find when you're looking closely.

We Need More Observations!

Once you've found as many creatures as you can, look at your list or your drawings and answer these questions:

❧ How many creatures did you find?

❧ Which ones were hard to see, and which were easy to see?

❧ Did any of the creatures have colors or patterns that looked like the things around them?

❧ Were the creatures moving quickly or sitting very still?

❧ Which creatures do you think were using camouflage?

❧ Why do you think those creatures were using camouflage?

Ask your assistant to help you search in a book or on the internet for the names of the creatures you found.

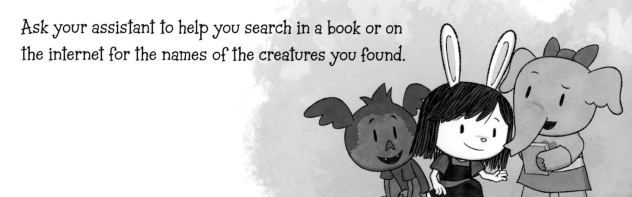

Also in the Elinor Wonders Why series

Elinor Wonders Why™

Forest Giants

Created by
Jorge Cham and Daniel Whiteson